HOSPITAL!

A Medical Satire of
Unhealthy Proportions

Kyle Bradford Jones

Black Rose Writing | Texas

First printing

This is a work of fiction. Names, characters, businesses,
places, events, and incidents are either the products of the
author's imagination or used in a fictitious manner. Any
resemblance to actual persons, living or dead, or actual
events is purely coincidental. The views and opinions
expressed in this book are those of the author and do not
necessarily reflect the official policy or position of the
author's employer, publisher or any parties mentioned
hereafter.

ISBN: 978-1-68513-090-9
PUBLISHED BY BLACK ROSE WRITING
www.blackrosewriting.com

Printed in the United States of America
Suggested Retail Price (SRP) $17.95

Hospital! is printed in Calluna

Anita,
stay cool + have a
great summer!

Kyle Jones

To Keanu Reeves. You know why.

Acknowledgements

I would like to thank the following people: my kids, from whom many of these ideas came. They are the most hiliariousest people I know. My wife, who puts up with all of my stupid jokes. The team at Black Rose Writing for publishing a silly book. My parents for birthing and raising me. My brother Tyler for introducing me to such ridiculous humor. My sister Keri for being my biggest fan. And to those readers who bought the book, because I need the money. But I'm not grateful to anyone else.

HOSPITAL!

This book was written
in front of a live studio audience.

Chapter One
Dr. Camus is a Jerk

When Dr. Camus powered down the hallway of The Peloton Forward Crescendo Care Amicus Health Priority Catalyst Wellness Code Blue Memorial Hospital of Her Motherly Excellence (slogan: "We are a hospital"), the tail of his rumpled white doctor's coat trailed behind him like the cape of an angry nineteenth-century magician. His short stature—no more than five-feet-five, though he claimed at least five-feet-nine—belied his scorn for humankind, instead of depicting a jolly elf-like demeanor typically expected of those without ample size. His entrance through the hospital lobby only worsened his mood, as the "fancy" player piano nearly constantly hit the wrong note, seeping further disorder and confusion into his perverse subconscious. Dr. Camus walked not only with a purpose, but with the explicit purpose of humiliating everyone possible in the wake of his ego; he intended to make everyone else pay for his own inadequacy and shortcomings (pun *intended*). Camus didn't just want you to know how much he despised you. It had to be joined with the absolute certainty that he was better than you in every way, even though he was a man of few genuine talents. He had trolled people for so long about the Monkees being more talented than the Beatles that he now *actually believed* it, and thus repeated it to anyone who wasn't listening. And, frankly, he also had a terrible haircut.

Dr. Camus didn't have the typical baggage of an egomaniacal archetype. No one abused him as a child. He didn't come from a broken home. No over-compensating to get his father's approval. He wasn't an alcoholic or drug addict. No broken marriages or other emotional traumas. He was simply a jerk. Nobody knew if he was always this way. I guess you'll just have to wait for the prequel.

His face was half-scowl and half-grin, like the scabrous predator that he was. He embodied all that was negative of a supposedly once noble profession, the tradition of which he openly mocked in the way he treated his "calling". He also refused to believe that he was ever actually called to such a vocation, a shocking disclosure to everyone in the old guard. No one even knew how he came to work at The Peloton Forward Care Crescendo Amicus Catalyst Health Priority Wellness Code Blue Memorial Hospital of Her Motherly Excellence; he simply kept showing up after his residency ended. It's unlikely that anyone would purposely *hire* him.

Someone at the nurse's station down the hall was smiling in anticipation of his arrival. She obviously didn't know him.

"Hello Dr. Camus, my name's Blanche. I'm caring for your patients in rooms 404 and 406."

Blanche was short but big-boned, a squat ball of sweetness and deference. She was fresh out of nursing school, eager to make a good first impression on the notorious Dr. Camus on the first day of her first job. He abruptly halted his squatty gait, as though interrupted by the unexpected sight of a dinosaur.

"Blanche? Your name is Blanche? What kind of [BLEEP] idiot names their kid Blanche?" he said to the poor nurse, who was now shaking in fright. "It sounds like someone [BLEEP] on the floor with a magic [BLEEP] in their [BLEEP]. Or like someone vomited up their stomach. No, no wait, it sounds more like a truck having a baby, stuck on the side of the road, the back fender creaking and cracking until out bursts a [BLEEP]-sized [BLEEP]. BLANCHE! BLANCHE!"

He made a motion as though he were vomiting, his shoulders rolling forward and head jutting out like a chicken (because evidently that is what a truck giving birth would look like).

"My...my...mother was a...a...*Golden Girls* fan..."

She hoped an explanation would calm him down, but he didn't even hear her. That was probably for the best.

The drab fluorescent lighting of the fourth floor of the mid-20th Century built hospital poisoned all reason and fed Camus's emotions. His personality also did that, but the venomous environment combined with his innermost self to create a positive (negative?) reinforcement loop that made him more monster than man. Blanche had heard he was an angry git (though since she wasn't British, she wasn't exactly sure what that meant) so tried to prepare herself for something quite horrific. She was nevertheless mortified by his completely callous disregard of decorum.

"And another thing [BLEEP] Broad Shoulders—my name is pronounced Cam-US, not Cam-OO. It's not French."

"Why does everyone think it's French?" he mumbled to himself.

Everyone else stared, anticipating a great show. One of the nursing aides used to make popcorn for everyone each morning while they watched an inevitable tirade against whoever raised Camus's ire, but after he burned a bag and the entire floor reeked of scorched earth, he was forced to stop. Not for any patient-safety reason, mind you, but just because it made its way into the administration suite, and they simply would not tolerate such odors. Yet somehow more popcorn appeared instantly. I never quite understood why the staff wore 3D glasses, though.

The only staff afraid of Dr. Camus were the new ones, those who had yet to meet him but had heard stories. The rest found him wholly obnoxious and yet strangely interesting. A few nurses who had worked at the hospital for more than a couple of years actually did an impressive impression of the cantankerous doctor. (It wasn't really that hard, just put together a bunch of BLEEPs in a row. Anyone can do it, really, though I would recommend the use of a censor.) They were still a bit uncomfortable when his indignation was aimed directly at them, but even then they found some perverse pleasure in the display.

The big problem (and also the biggest amusement) was that most of the time you had no idea what Camus was saying. His cursing curled the toes of the roughest sailor and stopped any soldiers in their tracks. His brand of swearing was to blend as many words together as possible, trying to achieve more emphasis out of the quantity of insults than the quality. This certainly seemed to mask the specific meaning of his diatribes, but still strongly emphasized his mindset. His goal was to be as scurrilous as possible to make others as uncomfortable and fearful as he was, though this wasn't a conscious realization to him. Interestingly, he really only pushed the patronizing if someone spoke to him; he was too self-pitying to start the process on his own, and actually preferred avoiding people whenever possible.

"Are my [BLEEP] patients okay or did you screw them up too, like your [BLEEP BLEEP] parents did with your name?" He continued. "Though I'm sure they were *lovely* people," he pinched out sarcastically.

"Um...well...they...uh..."

Blanche was already in the claw of terror and betrayal that everyone new to Dr. Camus entered. His dereliction of decency was deafening and defeated everyone in his path at first impression. (Sorry, alliteration with four words is a bit showy, but I couldn't help myself. After all, I, your humble narrator, am British.) Blanche was also very confused as to why there was a man following Dr. Camus, who blew an air horn every time he cursed.

"Well, what a [BLEEP] coinquidink! My father was a [BLEEP] celibate monk, but that didn't ruin my life! You know, you're just like every other nurse, lab technician, respiratory therapist, medical assistant, administrator, admissions specialist, secretary, doctor, resident, student, parking attendant, janitor, IT guy, receptionist, advanced practice clinician—and did I say administrator?—peon, moron, doltish spawn, and [BLEEP] rat in this place; a complete [BLEEP BLEEP]!"

While it would appear that the Censor was working overtime today with Camus, he had a lot of practice and was quite good at anticipating Camus's language.

Since he astutely negotiated payment for every BLEEP he had to use, he actually took home more income than any of the physicians. The administration figured it was cheaper to employ this guy—with full benefits as well, mind you—than to risk offending patients and staff, and thus creating even more lawsuits than Camus already inspired as it was. It is even to discourage you, dear reader, from suing the publisher of this story for excessive swearing. So please cut us some slack here— the Censor is very expensive.

Blanche burst into tears from this slanderous rant and ran off. Nobody blamed her, but nobody stood up for her either. Everyone sulked away, disappointed that there weren't more fireworks for the morning. Camus's behavioral dehiscence had been present for years, a stark contrast with some of the other clinicians on staff who were actually quite polite. He took pride in driving away nearly a dozen nurses and other staff to find employment elsewhere, even though he failed to see how the constant influx of raw hirelings actually made his life worse. He simply had no insight into how his behavior affected him, only how it affected others.

"You're doing quite well today, Censor," Dr. Camus said as an aside to his professional shadow.

The Censor was probably the only person who Camus actually respected, so good was he at his job. Not *liked,* but *respected.* He was also one of the few people who saw right through Camus's veneer to his black soul, finding nothing of substance remaining from his charred humanity. The moral injury of entering medicine was too much for Dr. Camus's sensitive psyche to handle, with everything he ever cared for crammed into the recesses of his subconscious. Hospital rumor was that he used to be a fairly likable fellow, but no one actually believed it. There is simply no appreciation of irony inside a hospital.

"Thanks. I've actually been considering shaking it up and using something other than 'BLEEP'," the Censor mused. "A different sounding horn, maybe? Or I could yell something like 'YEET'. The teenagers would love that one."

"Why mess with a [BLEEP] perfect system?" Camus retorted. He hated change. "It really is quite uncanny how you can predict my [BLEEP] cursing," Camus added in a moment of rarely seen sincerity.

"No, I'd say it's pretty canny. Quite canny, in fact," responded the Censor.

The thing with Dr. Camus (among many other "things") is that he wasn't that great of a doctor. He assumed he was, but he treated his patients the same way he treated everyone else—like a dirty urinal. Camus paid little attention to them and interacted with them as little as possible. He frequently left nothing more than a proverbial (and sometimes literal, come to think of it) urinal cake in their room without speaking to them, aside from an occasional incendiary invective. His diagnostic and treatment thoughts arose from an unknown ether that often had no relation to the patient. This was the major difference between him and any sort of medical television trope; on TV, hospitals tolerated dirt bag physicians because of their incredible intelligence. This confused everyone all the more as to why the administration permitted Camus's ongoing employment.

"This lady has pneumonoultramicroscopic-silicovolcanoniosis."

She didn't.

Camus yelled this to no one in particular but within earshot of everyone in the corridor, expecting someone to respond. He intended to confuse those not familiar with his favorite diagnosis, as the hospital was nowhere near a lung-damaging volcano. There is some question whether this is actually a diagnosis or simply a really long word to be used to impress people at cocktail parties. (I've certainly used it to some acclaim.)

"Start her on the usual treatment," he shouted to no one and everyone at once.

No one knew if the joke was against the patient, the staff, or himself, but it appeared he was starting to believe in his diagnostic prowess.

"Dr. Camus, that's the third case this week," stated Nurse Man. Camus didn't know any of the nurses' names (other than Blanche), and so made up a nickname for each of them. "Are you sure that's what's going on? This lady came in with abdominal pain, not anything respiratory."

Camus had somehow come across this "diagnosis" through a Wikipedia rabbit hole, and decided that more people would benefit from carrying that label. It was a process enviable to any millennial. No patient whom he had branded with this malady had similar symptoms to each other, but they tended to improve despite his efforts. He failed to grasp the biggest secret in medicine—99% of symptoms resolve without medical intervention. Granted, that one percent can be quite deadly (Dr. Camus only recently learned that being human has a 100% mortality rate), but thankfully, his patients were often more resilient than they should be. Perhaps out of necessity.

The staff adopted the notion that it was their job to protect the patients from him, which meant altering his orders or directly contradicting him to the patient's face. They gave him incomplete information to guide his behavior, hoping to spare the patients the same condescension that he doled out to everyone else. It was easy because the other hospitalists developed order sets for the nurses to use for various ailments in such cases.

But I digress. Everyone fell silent after Nurse Man's questioning, knowing the wrath immediately to follow from Camus. How dare someone question his authority and knowledge!? His expertise is second to none! (It's not, and he knew it on some subconscious level, but would never admit it to anyone, including himself.) Some of those around attempted to leave the area, though not far enough that they couldn't hear what he would say.

"Don't you dare [BLEEP] my amazing [BLEEP] wonder of science, my [BLEEP BLEEP] incredible, phenomenal, and imperturbable way of [BLEEP] song-like [BLEEP] until the pillow rips! I've seen a million patients and I've rocked them all! It's not my fault that there is an emetic of this stupid disease!"

"Don't you mean 'epidemic'?" the Censor quickly added.

Given his incorrect choice of words and astounding cursing pattern, no one knew what he was talking about, but the message was loud and clear. Except Nurse Man only smiled. He wasn't showing any signs of fear. He saw right through Camus's incompetence and toothless intimidation and met it with a sense of unflappability.

"You're such a cliché, Dr. Camus," said the nurse. He even pronounced the name Cam-MOO just to raise the doctor's indignation even further.

"What did you say?"

The excitement of the eavesdropping staff was snowballing.

"I said you're nothing but a cliché. Haven't you ever seen a medical TV show or movie? There's always the big [BLEEP BLEEP]..."

The Censor immediately apologized for assisting the nurse and let him continue.

"...who treats everyone else like garbage, like they're some sort of subhuman sausage that gets in the way of your supposed amazing power. You're completely absurd, Camus."

Nurse Man didn't know that we already exposited this a couple of pages ago. Also, Subhuman Sausage is a glorious name for a punk band.

"You think *I'm* a cliché? How many people here have a [BLEEP] podcast?" he asked the crowd. Three-fourths raised their hand. "And how many of you take an improv class?"

Approximately the same number of arms raised.

"Crap, I gotta get to class!" someone yelled in the back as they ran away.

"I rest my case," Camus said with a haughty bow.

Though it perplexed him that he had never thought of the name Subhuman Sausage, however.

Nurse Man continued, ignoring the ridiculous people in the crowd, mainly because their idiocy undermined his point: "But the main difference is that in the shows, the scumbag doctor is tolerated because of his brilliance, but you don't even have that. How are you even employed? The only thing that would make this dumb story even more of a cliché is if it were framed by you explaining the plot and character development to your psychiatrist."

The listening staff released an audible gasp in unison. Everything Nurse Man said was true, and they all knew it, but no one thought it would come out in such a direct way. And only a few among them realized the repetitive use of the word "cliché" here was in itself a cliché.

"What do you [BLEEP] mean? I'm definitely handsomer than Hugh Laurie!"

He wasn't. He figured that this non sequitur argument might make up for the insults about his inferior doctoring. And no one really understood why he assumed his looks were being attacked; his ugliness was a given. But why did he choose Hugh Laurie from *House, MD*?

"No one is more handsome than Laurie, I mean, come on. Maybe Jon Hamm, but you're far from him, too."

Everyone around was waiting for one of them to evoke George Clooney from *ER*, but it was far too obvious for either of them.

"Did Jon Hamm ever play a physician?" Camus couldn't recall any roles.

"At least once, but not well." Nurse Man had to focus to get his prior train of thought back on track. "I mean, pneumonoultra...whatever? What even is that?

The closest volcano is thousands of miles away and hasn't erupted in decades! Why in the world would we see a rash of such diagnoses in this area? It doesn't make any sense because IT'S A STUPID DIAGNOSIS!"

Phew, the nurse was even making me sweat a little. He surely was enjoying himself.

"And last week you diagnosed someone with 'migratory halitosis.' That doesn't even exist! It's not a thing!"

"He smelled everywhere," countered Camus.

But Nurse Man was not done.

"You're like the collar of a polo shirt that peeks over the neck of the sweater—it's useless AND pathetic! No, you're more like an actor at the time of his career when he can only get cheesy roles in terrible family movies, so you delude yourself that you accept these roles purely for the kids! You're as useless as the leftover sliver of soap in the shower. You're like...like...like a ship lost at sea that sinks because it's a dumb ship! Everyone loathes you, because all you do is insult and curse and harm patients and piss people off for no reason! I mean, how many assassination attempts have you avoided?"

That last line seemed especially harsh, but Camus had to admit that there were more than a few people who would prefer him dead.

"How out of touch can you really be? You probably think that Sting wrote a song about a stop light named Roxanne!"

"Well, I was recently elected into the Rock and Roll Hall of Fame."

It's true, Camus really was, despite no actual musical talent. But his petition to the Hall was pretty strong.

"I mean, take the frickin' blue pill and wake up already!" Yes, Nurse Man really said frickin'.

Camus was not used to open rebellion and thus didn't know how to respond, but the pill comment confused him.

"Don't you mean the green pill?" he said with scorn and more than a little curiosity.

"I'm pretty sure there wasn't even a green pill offered," replied an orderly, listening down the hall who now approached the argument. "I thought they were red and blue."

"No, I'm pretty sure it was pink," answered someone else.

"Why would it be pink? What's wrong with you?"

The conversation no longer belonged to Camus and the nurse, having been abruptly confiscated by the eavesdropping mass.

"It was a blue pill, but you're supposed to take the red one to see reality."

"What are you guys even talking about? What's the deal with the colored pills?" asked yet another onlooker.

"You know, in *Fight Club,* when the guy offers the other guy the opportunity to see what's really going on or continue on in ignorance?"

No one even recognized this guy, who was probably a patient's relative or something. No one else in a hospital would wear jeans with a button down and Birkenstock sandals with socks.

"It wasn't *Fight Club*, it was *The Matrix*." The head nurse, who barely arrived on the scene, knew enough of what was happening to correct the confused intruder, but not enough to avoid confusing everyone else. "Keanu has to decide if he'll accept Samuel L. Jackson's offer to leave the matrix."

Multiple others chimed in on their thoughts of who the actor *actually* was as the discussion quickly escalated to bigger issues. The group of people were so engrossed that no one even noticed the patient who was on fire run down the hall and jump out the window.

"It's not Samuel L. Jackson! It's Mario van Peebles!"

"van Peebles hasn't been in anything in decades! And they don't even look alike. How could you possibly think it was him?"

"I could have sworn it was Wesley Snipes. Remember him? That dude was KILLER!"

"Now you're all just throwing out random black dudes. It was actually Denzel. You're all nothing more than a bunch of racists."

"Just because I don't know which actor did what doesn't make me racist!"

"Well, you didn't bother to find out, did you?"

"I've never even seen this movie!"

"What, you refuse to watch movies with black people in them?"

"I'm so confused," said more than one person to themselves.

So many people had been blurting out nonsense that no one even knew who said what, but it's safe to say that what started out as an exposition of Camus in our brief story was now something entirely different. Nurse Man and Camus had said nothing since the pill discussion went off the rails and just watched in an unamused torpor. Only the new medical student who hadn't figured out which doctor he was supposed to work with was still concerned about the accuracy of the pill's color.

"It's white! That's the only color that matters! All of these other colors are completely ridiculous! No other colors even make sense. How could you all be so stupid?" he yelled out in a sudden moment of quiet.

Everyone whipped their heads around and looked at him in confusion, disbelief, and utter silence. They didn't realize that he was still talking about the pill's color, and he did not know they were talking about skin color. He didn't get why everyone was now looking at him in shock and disdain.

"What?" he embarrassingly stated.

He slowly backed away as tears filled his eyes. As he ran away, he mumbled something about how stupid he was because he still got the color wrong. Everyone quickly turned away from him to continue scolding each other.

"How in the world did this get to be about race?"

"This chubby moron has no idea that there is more than one black man in Hollywood, and Mister Future Doctor Scumbag, who ran away, is dumb enough to blurt out his own thoughts on skin color."

This might be a good time to point out that everyone currently engaged in this mess was white; the token African-American employee in this suburban hospital had the day off.

One person knelt on one knee as though the national anthem were playing. Someone else raised a fist in solidarity with...something. She didn't even know what it meant. It merely felt like something she should do.

"Did you really think that since I got the actor wrong, that means I have no respect for black people? No one has more respect for them than me! My best friend in junior high was black."

He then dramatically dropped a microphone, which seemed to materialize out of nowhere. He thought his last comment proved without a doubt that his views were pure.

Even Dr. Camus didn't tackle such controversial subjects as race relations. He preferred to discuss abortion.

"Oh sure, rain on the race parade! Pretty soon you're all gonna be raggin' on gays, too." It appeared the crowd wanted to step this up a notch. "Why ain't we talking about *Milk*, man, instead of the stupid Keanu movie? Harvey'll show us the way! And besides, why does 'Word' insist on knowing my orientation before I change the page layout?! What if my sexual orientation doesn't fit a specific category, and THEN what? Huh, Bill Gates?! This world is ridiculous!"

"Why would we talk about the milkman? Besides, my milk 'man' is a woman, so don't get me started on all of your sexist statements over the years."

"Um, should we be talking about all of this?" one random guy asked innocuously.

No one heard him as all the comments quickly became unidentifiable as each voice raised to stand out above another.

"Do you wanna go get a beer?" Camus asked Nurse Man quietly under the rising din of the debate all around them.

Nurse Man looked at his watch: 9:10am.

"Yeah, sure, why not?"

No one noticed as they discreetly slipped away.

Chapter Two
Dr. Camus Remains a Jerk

"Listen, you [BLEEP] worthless tubby," Dr. Camus began with one [BLEEP] poor patient in a hospital bed. [Censor's note: Please forgive me, I'm not supposed to help the narrator. Sometimes I just get [BLEEP] carried away.] "I don't like you and you don't like me. So let's get this over with. You look like a [BLEEP] whale, you smell like a donkey that died in the [BLEEP] bowels of a latrine, and it's only a matter of time until this all kills you. We'll start by giving you a 500 calorie-a-day diet while you're here so you can start to lose some [BLEEP BLEEP] flab, and then...wait...why are you here exactly?"

"I'm getting a new knee," the patient squeaked with eyes full of fear.

"Oh, you're a [BLEEP BLEEP BLEEP] turf from orthopedics?! And now I have to manage your [BLEEP] diabetes and [BLEEP] heart failure just for them, huh?! Unbelievable. Those [BLEEP] turtle necks need to

[BLEEP] a new [BLEEP BLEEP] until it falls out of the sky! I deserve to be paid extra to deal with your [BLEEP BLEEP]."

The patient didn't know what to say. He was already scared to be in the hospital, was worried about his surgery, and had been told that he was at high risk for complications. He had a huge deductible on his insurance plan but had no idea how he would meet it, as he frequently missed work because of his health problems. His only family was an estranged son, the stress of loneliness being the ultimate cause of his overeating. He was fighting back tears as it was, even without the berating from this doctor he barely met who passed fiery judgement on him. Camus viewed himself almost as a priest, the patient's history a confessional, but one that he didn't want to deal with. He didn't care to listen, absolve, or forgive, but only to exert his power of indifference.

And just as a Mephistophelian grin appeared on Dr. Camus's face, he bolted out of the room, leaving a startled and apprehensive patient to grieve his lot in life.

"How many patients do we have on this floor that are just waiting for an orthopedic surgery?" Camus yelled at the closest nurse.

"Probably about half," answered Nurse Know-It-All, who didn't even really act as though she knew it all. That's simply how Dr. Camus chose to see her.

The Censor knew Camus was on a tear and that only more cursing was coming, but it was at this precise moment that his air horn broke.

"OH NO OH NO OH NO NO NO NO NO NO!" the Censor shrieked in terror. "The horn is broken! We're at DEFCON level 1 here! Camus, you can't curse AT ALL for the next few minutes! I usually carry an extra, but I left it in my other pants."

"Come on, man! I'm just getting started yelling at the nurse! And I'm pretty sure you mean DEFCON level 5? I think that's the worst one."

"Oh, not now Camus!"

And Camus was wrong, anyway. Camus turned his attention back to Nurse Know-It-All to resume his prior questioning. It took every cell in his body to avoid cursing.

"And what about drunks or druggies detoxing, chronic pelvic pain, or fatties that smell like...like...really bad?"

"Everyone but Mrs. Ogilvie in 403. She's the one with the bowel obstruction."

"Unbelievable," Camus mumbled to himself as he stormed off. "Good, now they'll have a nice variety of patients. It's about time those orthopedists got a taste of their own medicine." Camus wished more had heard his retort, even though it wouldn't make much sense to anyone yet.

• • •

"Wait a minute, what is this? Are you kidding me, Camus?!" Dr. Sapient could not believe her eyes. Dr. Camus had transferred Mrs. Ogilvie to the orthopedic service.

"Camus, I don't know how to treat a bowel obstruction! I don't even know how to treat acne. How am I supposed to care for this woman? She needs an actual doctor, not someone who spends her day building erector sets in the OR!"

"Ever tried looking in a book, you lazy [BLEEP]?" retorted Dr. Camus. Thankfully, the Censor had fixed his air horn in the nick of time to resume his duties. "You better get used to it because you're getting a bunch of my favorite [BLEEP] patients now! Do you know how to handle heroin addicts with 'abdominal pain'? Well, get ready!"

Dr. Camus was so proud of himself for thinking of this. It was well past due. He was sick of having to take care of all the medical problems of hospital patients awaiting or recovering from an orthopedic surgery. Why should only ortho be allowed to cherry-pick patients in the hospital?

• • •

Camus quickly decided to take the issue one step further. He went to the Chief Medical Officer of The Peloton Health Forward Crescendo Care Priority Amicus Catalyst Wellness Code Blue Memorial Hospital of Her Motherly Excellence —the Godfather. Some even called him The Don, though that was more because his name was actually Don than any clever nickname given his stature in the medical community. He carried himself in a way to appear dignified, august, and even accessible, though it came across more as aloof and ineffectual. His use of obscure vocabulary further distanced himself from his colleagues, though was a source of immense pride to him. He even developed a faux British accent to add an element of esteem. And yet he wanted to be approachable, thus encouraging people to call him Don instead of Dr. Doff. Few knew how long he had been at The Peloton Health Forward Crescendo Care Priority Amicus Catalyst Wellness Code Blue Memorial Hospital of Her Motherly Excellence, but presumably long enough to see the multitude of mergers and sponsorships over the years that added a new word or two to the title each time.

"Don, I've had it with these boring, mundane, banal patients that constantly come through these doors," Camus complained.

"Well hello Lou, it's good to see you. Excellent use of 'banal', by the way. I'm thoroughly bedazzled. And I'm much obliged to you for bowdlerizing your germinal sentence to me."

Camus wasn't sure why Dr. Doff called him Lou; it wasn't his name now, nor was it ever.

"What in the world does 'bowdlerize' mean?"

"To expurgate your words."

"I still don't follow you, Don."

"You know, to lustrate."

Camus simply stared at him, adding an exasperated flinch, implying that The Don was being a [BLEEP].

"To censor."

"Oh, I get it. Well, the Censor's at lunch, so my vocabulary is pretty limited for the moment."

"So it is. To which cases do you refer?"

The Don was willing to listen to Camus, though at this point he had no intention of doing anything about his complaint.

"I'm not going to see these disgusting patients anymore. No fatties, no slobs, no homeless, no drunks, no heroin addicts, none of these animals. I've had it! They're so relentless and annoying. There's no challenge. What about the good ol' days when we used to see the diagnostic puzzles, the people who had actual problems?" Camus was trying to show deference to his superior, because that was the only way to appease The Don.

"You do recognize that those cases provide over 50% of our revenue?"

Whenever revenue, or margin, or profit, or any other business-related term came in, the individuals in question were no longer referred to as "patients," but something like "cases" or "bodies" or, The Don's personal favorite, "consumers."

"I don't care about revenue! I care about taking care of patients!" yelled Camus in mock righteous indignation.

He didn't care about patients. No one really knew what he cared about, least of all himself.

"I believe that the 'good ol' days' to which you refer occurred during your residency when your attendings mostly assigned you the stimulating learning cases; they shielded you from the dross for purposes of erudition, and now it's time to care for whoever comes in, no matter how recrementitious they may be." The Don was fully utilizing his thesaurus study today.

"I can't do this anymore, Don. This is killing me. Where are the actual patients?"

By "real", he superficially meant those that didn't smell, which would only leave roughly 2-3% of all hospitalized patients. If he had access to his subconscious mind, he would realize that what he truly meant deep down was those who had no possibility of dying on him.

"They procure care up yonder at the Good Hospital."

They did.

"Well, I can't do this! This is ridiculous. I'll just have to go work at the 'good hospital,'" Camus surmised.

"First of all, the Good Hospital does not reside in quotations; its appellation originates from Dr. Good, its adroit founding physician."

Camus rolled his eyes at The Don's clarification, even though it was an interesting tidbit he hadn't known.

"And second," The Don continued, "you know you lack the sagacity to take your employ to such an esteemed bastion of healing, anyway. You're actually quite fortunate to be *here.*"

Camus knew that deep down. His internal mental defenses kept the truth from his conscious mind, all in the name of ego. Even his subconscious knew the danger of offending his ego.

"Okay, well, then I'll turf all of my cases to orthopedics. They'll finally get a taste of their own medicine, if they even know what medicine is."

"Such dealings have already made their way to me. While we're going to have to put a stop to your orthopedic rascality, I understand your perturbation. But you're just going to have to accept my injunction to cease such untoward comportment."

"But Sapient said I look like an alien donkey."

She wasn't wrong, but The Don wasn't listening. He headed to the door, but turned back dramatically with a piece of perceived sage advice.

"Remember—helping people doesn't just mean ameliorating the health of those of whom you are fond. It also means helping any spavined plebeian." He winked and left the room.

Since Camus hated everybody and had a fairly limited vocabulary, he didn't know what The Don was talking about.

· · · ·

"I had the weirdest dream last night," began Karen.

"Oh really? What was it?"

The burly unit coordinator, Flo, wasn't interested. (Camus didn't know if either of those names were correct, but he called them that because...well...he just did.) Any typical person would pickup on the annoyance in her tone, except Karen. She was a middle-aged blonde nurse who was more interested in talking than doing her job, and chafed anytime someone accused her of not working. Karen always had a story that no one wanted to hear, and press-on nails that broke every hygiene protocol in the hospital. She also made it very apparent that she was always chewing gum.

"So there I was, listening to Captain and Tenille," she began as Camus walked by.

He stopped mid-stride.

"Ugh, are you [BLEEP] kidding me? First, ALL dreams are weird. There has never been a [BLEEP] un-weird dream in the history of humanity. Unless there were red drapes and a [BLEEP] dancing midget, then no one wants to hear about your brand of weird." Camus was in a decent mood, so he continued offering his unsolicited advice.

"What? A dancing midget? What are you talking about?"

"You're obviously too basic to understand the reference," he said with a snide elevation of his eyebrows, even though he knew no pop culture references since the nineties.

"And second, NEVER start a story with 'so there I was.' That immediately tells you that there is nothing, even REMOTELY [BLEEP] interesting coming and so all listeners should just [BLEEP] walk away. Any dunce knows that.

"And third of all, do you really listen to [BLEEP BLEEP] Captain and Tennille unironically? How is that even possible? Don't you know the rules of 1970s yacht rock? The rule is DON'T. There is simply no [BLEEP] excuse."

"The Captain just happens to be my uncle," Karen replied with misplaced pride.

He wasn't.

"Wait a minute, did I hear you correctly? THE CAPTAIN is your *uncle*? What were family reunions like growing up? Did he have any [BLEEP] pet muskrats he mated together? Did he serenade you all? He has to be the [BLEEP] creepiest looking musician ever!"

Camus waited for a response, but since Karen had made it all up, he grunted and left.

"You know, you fustrate me so much, you big jerk!" Karen yelled at him as he walked away.

Camus stopped in his tracks yet again, cocked his head slightly to one side, and wrinkled his brow.

"Yeah, you heard me!" she added to emphasize her point.

"Did you say 'fustrate'? Did you REALLY just say 'fustrate'?"

"Yeah, why? Is that a problem?"

"Who in the [BLEEP BLEEP] says 'fustrate'? Are you going to the 'libary' after work? What possible [BLEEP] reason would there be to remove the most critical letter from that word? No one with half a brain EVER says 'fustrate'. I bet you talk to strangers on [BLEEP BLEEP] elevators, don't you?!"

Karen ignored Camus's taunts and turned back to Flo.

"You are some piece of [BLEEP] work! Aren't you also the nurse who claims to predict urinalysis results just by looking at it? You're just as creepy as that

[BLEEP] uncle of yours. You know, you're like those classic rock songs that are remade by some [BLEEP] breathy woman at about five times slower than the original—only there to annoy the [BLEEP] out of everyone! Just go back to your glutton-free diet."

"You mean gluten?"

"Whatever!"

Camus resumed his hasty cadence down the hallway, shaking his head, even looking back once in disbelief.

"Anyway, as I was saying, so there I was."

Given the opening from Camus, Flo felt confident speaking up.

"Wait, wait. I hate siding with Dr. Camus on anything, but he's right. You need to find a different opening. And The Captain *is* really creepy."

Karen showed her offense and disgust. There she was, just trying to tell the story of her peculiar—but interesting! definitely still interesting—dream, and now she was defending herself from these ungrateful cretins.

"Oh, well, in that case, I won't even tell you."

She turned her back to Flo to emphasize her hurt feelings.

"Fine, just tell me."

Having said her piece to no avail, Flo grasped her prior detached attitude.

"Okay. So there I was…"

•

"Hey Camus!" Dr. Sapient yelled as she spotted him in the cafeteria. "Guess what?"

"What—you realized you look like a [BLEEP] terrorist in your surgical mask and so you've decided to kidnap me?"

Camus didn't even realize how racist that was, so proud was he of his new put down.

Dr. Sapient's head slightly recoiled with a furrowed brow.

"No, I...What?...Do I really look like a terrorist?"

"Yes, you [BLEEP] dolt, you do."

He was just trying to get back at her for the "alien donkey" remark.

"And why are you carrying your [BLEEP] hands out in front of you like that?" Camus would not quit.

"I just washed them. I don't want to contaminate them again!"

"It looks like you're heading in to [BLEEP] surgery! Normal people don't walk around like they're entering a [BLEEP] OR."

"Okay, well, whatever. I cured Ms. Ogilvie!" Sapient was very proud of herself.

"Who?"

Camus had a habit of not knowing anyone's name, no matter how often he interacted with them.

"You know, that patient you gave me this morning?"

"Wait, how did you cure her? She had a severe blockage and you don't know anything about *real* medical problems."

"Well, once I examined her, I realized she was presenting with Ogilvie Syndrome after her recent heart surgery," said Sapient smugly.

Dr. Camus didn't want her to know that he didn't have a clue what Ogilvie Syndrome was.

"Oh, well, sure, Ogilvie Syndrome. Makes perfect sense. I'm pretty sure I told you that when I [BLEEP] transferred her to you."

Camus refused to look her in the eye, lest she discern how clueless he was. But Sapient wasn't stupid and quickly picked up on Camus's avoidance.

"You don't even know what Ogilvie Syndrome is, do you?"

"Sure I do. I see it all the time. It's easy to diagnose, even easier to treat! You simply have to know how to recognize it, especially after something like heart surgery."

Camus was stabbing in the dark—he wasn't really sure how or if the heart surgery played a role.

"Don't worry, I'll spare you the embarrassment," Sapient spoke with a tone of condescension that she had clearly earned. "You know, when you have an acute colonic dilation, often after a major surgery. The exam fit the picture, the history was a slam dunk, and I just looked at the x-ray. Did you even know there *was* a x-ray?"

"Of course I did! It wasn't a conclusive image!"

Camus was defensive, but also a bit perturbed that Sapient had disrupted his lunch. He was hungry. And he didn't know how to read x-rays.

"Besides, her last name *is Ogilvie!* They named the syndrome after her grandfather! What are the odds? She actually mentioned it to me as a possible diagnosis. All you had to do was listen to her. She might have died if she stayed in your care."

"So what did you [BLEEP] do about it?"

Camus pretended like he was indulging her in explaining her treatment, but he was actually very curious.

"Essential oils," Dr. Sapient said matter-of-factly.

Camus began laughing, not the type where he was tickled by a funny joke, but more the type where he really, *really* wanted you to know that he was laughing *at* you.

"You've got to be joking? Essential [BLEEP] oils? Did you make a poultice or a balm? Did you spill a rat's entrails to divine the appropriate remedy? How in the [BLEEP] world would that [BLEEP] treat [BLEEP] Ogilvie Syndrome? Explain such [BLEEP] witchcraft!"

"You've just gotta know the right mix. I can actually cure a lot of fractures with them, too."

"Ugh, you're so erotic," answered Camus mistakenly.

The Censor immediately elbowed him, quite hard in fact, right in the ribs, and whispered quite loudly, "I think you mean 'neurotic.'"

He definitely meant "neurotic", but he couldn't go back now. Camus became more serious as he realized that his plan of humiliating the orthopedic surgeons was blowing up in his face.

"But how did it work so quickly? It was only a few hours ago that you got her."

"That's just how good I am," she said, with more than a hint of pride and satisfaction.

Camus stared blankly into space with his mouth agape and brow furrowed as she walked away. He could not believe his bad luck. Camus just wanted to get away from seeing dumb patients and figured he might have a case if he showed how unique he was in the problems he could treat, except that the orthopedist *and* the patient were even better at internal medicine than he was. He was doomed to see the bottom of society's barrel day in and day out.

But just then his eyebrows raised a bit in concert with his mood. He had figured out his next step to avoid seeing the patients he so hated.

Chapter Three
Dr. Camus is Still a Jerk

"What have you [BLEEP] got for me now?"

Camus was calling the Emergency Department after being paged for an admission.

"I got five fer ya, ya lazy suckah," answered Dr. Reggie.

No one knew Reggie's last name, and his outer shell was just enough of a façade to keep superficial people from knowing him at all. But everyone in the hospital that cared to, saw his underlying goodness, so took all of his outward grumpiness in stride, except for Camus. He hated Reg, seeing in him competition for the hearts and minds of the hospital's inhabitants. He didn't like Reg's accent, mostly because everyone else found it charming. (No one even knew where his accent came from. Some said Australia, some said Moldova, and some swore that it was from New Jersey.) He didn't like how Reg said certain things—instead of saying NSAIDs or anti-inflammatories, he always said the entire name, non-steroidal anti-inflammatory medication. ("Has dat payshent tried non-steroidal anti-inflammatory medicashun?") Reg gave Camus as much as Camus gave anyone else. Camus thus considered Reg's façade as a lack of sincerity, and thus morally inferior to his own petulance and unfair to his own well-being. This all added up to make Reg the only person who *really* got under Camus's skin.

"Five?! Are you kidding me? What type of [BLEEP BLEEP] window [BLEEP] are you [BLEEP BLEEP BLEEP] do you see [BLEEP] rubber ball [BLEEP BLEEP] Post-It Notes!"

Dr. Reggie really had no idea what this all meant, but he loved the reaction.

"Yah! Instead of complainin', ya shud problee joost git down here and take care a' these poor peeple. I got two drunks tha' need ta' soober up, some ol' lady with a broken lig and pneumonia, and two yung gents wit sum pain in their billies. Come git at it, you wretch." Dr. Reggie hung up smiling, delighting in the abuse he flung at Camus.

"Well, here's my [BLEEP] chance," thought Camus.

The Censor had become so good in the last few months that he could even insert his work into Camus's thoughts.

As Camus entered the ED, Reg caught him.

"And bekuz I like you so mech, you can alsoo admeet za psych guy over dar'. He tried to keel heemself by leavin' za cah on in hees garage. But it deedn't work bekuz it was an eelectreek cah!" Reg roared with laughter.

Camus wasn't even sure if the patient was real or Reg was just cracking a joke, though he did find it quite funny.

"Well, it's not like I'm doing anything with these patients anyway," Camus mumbled to himself.

Camus walked straight into ED room 101 to see the first of the now six patients he was to admit.

"Mr. Johnson, is it? Well, keep quiet you [BLEEP], I don't really care what's going on with you. I need you to get your clothes on and come with me."

Mr. Johnson was groggy and still quite drunk. He wasn't sure where he was, but he was coherent enough to know that he couldn't get his pants on by himself.

"Grrgghew…I neehgad…fulmbiy…" was all he could get out.

"Come on, Mr. Johnson, I don't have all day."

Camus kept looking through the door to make sure no one was watching what he was doing. So far, the coast was clear.

Mr. Johnson pointed to his pants as he rolled onto his side on the bed from his sitting position.

"Okay, okay."

Camus didn't understand Mr. Johnson's efforts to communicate, but decided it would take too long to get him dressed.

"Forget about putting these on now. Just get in the wheelchair," said Camus hastily.

Camus grabbed the bag of clothes and wheeled Mr. Johnson towards the Exit. He nonchalantly said to no one in particular, "Just taking him out for a smoke." No one noticed or cared.

"Well Mr. Johnson, this is where it ends." Camus dumped his patient out of the wheelchair into the flower garden on the side of the hospital. "Here are your clothes. You'll be fine, just don't drink anymore for a few hours and then...well, whatever."

Mr. Johnson peered at the doctor with paranoia and confusion that Camus had kicked him out of the hospital.

"Okay, one down, five left to go."

No one picked up on Camus's plan until the third patient was gone. Nurse Annoying (Camus was truly convinced that was her name) began poking around.

"Dr. Camus, where is Mr. Johnson? I didn't see anyone take him upstairs to his room, and he hasn't been back in here since his smoke break."

Camus was exasperated. "Nurse, I don't know where he is. Am I my patient's keeper? He's probably in the bathroom or something. I don't keep a constant [BLEEP] watch on him. As you can see, I'm hard at work admitting these [BLEEP BLEEP] patients."

The nurse kept her eyes suspiciously narrow even as she shrugged it off.

"Well, he's not my patient, I guess," she justified.

Besides dumping Mr. Johnson outside, he called a Lyft to pick up one of the young men with abdominal pain and take him home. He assumed that the patient was faking it to get opioids, but if Camus had actually examined him and looked at his vitals, he may have recognized the signs of appendicitis. Fortunately, this gentleman didn't die, because his friend took him to a different hospital a couple of hours later, where they rushed him into emergency surgery.

The other twenty-something man really *was* looking for opioids, but Camus turfed him to a surgeon for admission, citing all the wonderful surgical goodness that could be hiding within that painful abdomen. Though Camus never found out, they took the patient to the OR for an exploratory surgery that found nothing. They sent him home with some OxyContin and a killer new scar.

Camus still had three patients to deal with. First, the old gomer with a broken hip and pneumonia. She was near the end, for sure. An elderly person breaking their hip is often a first sign of the end coming quickly. The fact that she had pneumonia (which probably led to the fall that broke her hip) made it even worse. Deep down, Camus hated death.

"Nurse Annoying! Get me the number for Dr. Doktore."

Dr. Doktore was a renowned orthopedic surgeon at the Good Hospital up the street.

"But what about Dr. Sapient or the other orthopedists here? Why do you need to talk to Dr. Doktore?"

She was catching on that Camus wasn't actually admitting any of these patients, only getting rid of them. It was personal survival, but also getting back at the hospital for the perceived poor treatment of him for years. The best form of revenge was sending private insurance money to their chief competitor.

"Please, are you a [BLEEP] doctor? Don't question me, just get me the [BLEEP] number."

"No, unless you explain to me what you're doing." The nurse had her arms folded with a defiant air that said, 'I'm not afraid of you and will happily bring you down.'

"Look, the place where this old [BLEEP] lady broke her hip is very unusual and will require a complicated procedure to fix. Our surgeons here simply aren't equipped to handle it."

Camus did his best to act as though this was for the patient's own good, and thanks to his disdain, it actually *was* for her own good.

"Alright fine. But you owe me flowers. And some chocolates. Dinner at a fancy restaurant for me and someone else who is not you. And at least a hundred dollars in cash! I'm watching you!"

"Yeah, yeah, whatever, just give me the [BLEEP] number." Camus dialed and lowered his voice to avoid anyone overhearing the call.

"Yeah, hi Dr. Doktore."

"It's not pronounced 'doctor', it's doc-TOR-A. It's French," Dr. Doktore corrected.

"I would've guessed Eastern European, but whatever," Camus answered apathetically.

"FRENCH!"

"Okay, yeah, um, sorry, I get it. French. Listen, I've gotta great [BLEEP]...oh, sorry...patient for you that can use your expertise."

After Camus told him about the patient, Doktore was quite confused.

"Why are you calling me? Why in the world are you suggesting a transfer? Dr. Sapient is more than competent to handle this."

"Yes, well, she and I don't exactly see eye-to-eye on certain things, if you know what I mean. I really think that this patient would receive better care in your hands."

"Why? Because she's a woman?"

"You said it, not me."

But that was part of it. Never mind that Dr. Sapient was an infinitely better doctor than Camus in every way.

"This patient has ASL, so we're not equipped for it."

"ASL? Do you mean 'ALS'?"

"Whatever," mumbled Camus sheepishly.

"Hm. Well, alright, I guess I'll take her. Have your staff handle the details and I'll prep our staff for a direct admit. But one more thing."

"Yeah?" Camus responded.

"Never call me again. You disgust me."

"Uh, yeah, sure, okay."

Camus was delighted and relieved, even despite Doktore's annoyance with him. His plan was working! He figured that the hospital would now realize how vital he was, but every reasonable person understood the opposite was happening.

What Camus did not realize was that Dr. Reggie was standing behind him and listening to the call.

"Vat err yu doin', yu [BLEEP BLEEP]? Yu cant du zat! Shee needs ta bee hare, not at ze Gude Haspitall! Yer go-an dawn, Kamoo!"

The Censor apologized for BLEEPing Reg. "Force of habit."

"It's pronounced Cam-US!" yelled Camus as he finally snapped, taking out his fury on anything within reach. "It's NOT FRENCH!"

Free pharmaceutical pens flew in all directions, a mug of coffee shattered against the wall, a cat was kicked into a hospital volunteer with a thud and a yowl, and an intern was punched in the nose. After looking around for something else to attack, Camus flipped over a stool like a clown forcefully emptying a wheelbarrow.

As if right on cue, Rosencrantz, the hospital CEO, arrived at just the wrong moment.

• • •

"Camus, this time you've gone too far," began Rosencrantz the CEO, as he berated Camus in his luxurious office.

"Have I? Or is this one of those moments when you arrive after we haven't seen each other in a really long time to tell me dramatically that you're [BLEEP] dying?"

"Oh no, don't change the subject on me!" Rosencrantz the CEO would not be fooled again.

[Narrator's aside: Rosencrantz the CEO's contract states that the author has to include his title as often as possible. And since brevity is the soul of all funny things, I will do my best to stay within legal compliance of all requests as much as possible heretofore throughout the entirety of this tale. Though I also might not. It depends how I feel.]

Rosencrantz the CEO tried to make himself look livid, but in reality, he didn't really care that much. The dark features upon his lilywhite skin, his razor that was perpetually stuck on the "Sexy" setting for the perfect length of beard scruff, and perfectly coiffed black hair with minimal product meant he had leeway to do nearly whatever he wanted. Despite his Ivy League education, his intellect was more equal to the village idiot than any grand master. His success came from his looks, his connections, a slightly above-average charm, and growing up in great wealth.

"Wait...what did you do this time again?" Rosencrantz the CEO asked sincerely, but with bite.

He couldn't stop thinking about his new Porsche and thus quickly lost his train of thought with Camus.

"You tell me. I'm only doing what you pay me to do."

"Right, right. How much do we pay you, again?"

Rosencrantz the CEO realized he could use disciplinary action to save the hospital some money, by which he actually meant "save the shareholders and himself" some money.

"Does it really matter? Just slap my wrist and let me [BLEEP] get outta here."

"Come on Camus, aren't you supposed to be the Chosen One? You know, the prophecy made by the hospital's founder, Mr. Motherly Excellence?"

"No, you're thinking of Phil."

"Oh, that's right. I like Phil. That makes a lot more sense. Have you met his new wife? She's so great. Donated a lot of money at our fundraiser last year." Rosencrantz the CEO had quickly gone off topic, as he was wont to do. He suddenly snapped back to the previous conversation. "Your behavior this time calls for a much bigger punishment than what you've received in the past."

"Yeah? What are you gonna do, take off your belt, daddy?"

Camus knew that his only hope for leniency was to keep distracting Rosencrantz the CEO; this technique had saved him from more severe punishments in the past. But once Rosencrantz the CEO started talking about money and suspension, Camus's hopes vanished.

"We are suspending you without pay for one month while you undergo anger management therapy."

'Boy, the Board will *love* this!' thought Rosencrantz the CEO.

He was quite proud of himself for coming up with this. And on the spot, no less! He really did deserve a raise, you know.

"WHAT?! You can't do that, you [BLEEP BLEEP] sack of [BLEEP BLEEP] with a [BLEEP] forehead!" Camus said.

It wasn't true, though—Rosencrantz the CEO had an exquisite forehead.

Camus was getting so creative with his cursing that the Censor even considered using the Shifted symbols above the numbers on the keyboard for the text instead of the [BLEEP]s, but for now the air horn was much simpler for him and the transcriber. Despite Camus's rage, Camus really couldn't help but be pleased with himself for his new linguistic concoctions.

"Look, it's the only way you'll learn."

Rosencrantz the CEO loved the power and authority this gave him. He never would have guessed that an MBA was more powerful than an MD. The pen is mightier than the scalpel...or something.

"You think that just because you have a [BLEEP] MBA that you're more powerful than an MD?! You think you can [BLEEP] tell me what to do? Ohhhh, you are SORELY mistaken you [BLEEP BLEEP] tool of the [BLEEP] pajamas with feet!"

"Camus, you better stop talking like this or I'll..."

"Or you'll what? Fire me? You can't fire me, Rosie! I'm the only non-idiot that works in this place! You think you can run this [BLEEP] hospital with the loonies you have here? This is such a cliché! You don't have the power to get rid of me!"

Camus was right, Rosencrantz the CEO couldn't go that far without the Board's approval, but given the number of infractions against him, it wouldn't be *that* hard.

"I've stood up for you before," remarked Rosencrantz the CEO. "Remember that suit because you wrote 'FU SOB' on the patient's discharge instructions? I battled for you and we won."

"You weren't standing up for *me*, you were standing up for the [BLEEP BLEEP] hospital! And besides, that's medical lingo for 'Follow up shortness of breath'."

Truthfully, Camus didn't remember this event.

"Well, the patient didn't know that!" crowed Rosencrantz the CEO.

"I've never been [BLEEP] negligible, you know that."

"Don't you mean 'negligent'? And yes, you have, actually, been both negligible and negligent."

"Well, what I lack in talent, I certainly make up for in [BLEEP] stage presence."

Rosencrantz the CEO had pretty much ignored every complaint against Camus since he arrived as CEO a few years earlier, except for the malpractice claims. He truly could not care less about what happened to the patients or staff. He just wanted to look good in front of his superiors. His goal was to be the CEO of not merely the hospital, but the mammoth conglomerate that owned this and thousands of other hospitals around the country. That would make him the most powerful man in private health care. Camus was no more than a gnat in his way, but Rosencrantz the CEO decided to pull out the bazooka this time to show his creativity in fiscal responsibility.

"The problem is that the hospital simply can't afford typical intensive anger management therapy for you," Rosencrantz the CEO said as he put his custom-made Sutor Mantellassi-shoed feet on the mammoth, imported-mahogany desk that consumed less than one-sixteenth of his office.

[Narrator's aside: In case you don't understand what the previous sentence says about this character, it means that he wore very expensive clothes, had a large, exquisite desk, and had an enormous office. I mean, come on, do I have to spell out everything? Really? Do you know how hard it is to be a narrator?! It's my responsibility to ensure that every single one of you understands what's happening, especially in this absurd story. Just meet me halfway, that's all I ask...for now.]

"Wait, are you telling me that even with the one month's worth of my salary that you are getting back, you still can't pay for the treatment that you're forcing me to have? So am I supposed to pay for it myself?"

Camus had calmed down, but more out of pure shock and disbelief than any control of his emotions. It was as though he was drowning, getting to the point of submission instead of fighting against his hated rival.

"No, you won't have to pay for it yourself, though that is a strong option I hadn't considered. We're going to have to send you to a hypnotist."

Rosencrantz the CEO's pride was growing by the second; he couldn't restrain the smile he had. This was even better than convincing the board to fire Camus, spending a year to find a replacement who would then take another year just to get used to how the hospital ran, and slowly develop the same attitude and behavior as this stupid doctor. He knew this from experience.

"A hypnotist?" Had Rosencrantz the CEO lost it? "Have you lost it? How does that even work?"

"Oh, it'll work. There's actually a lot of science that hypnosis can solve serious behavioral issues."

Rosencrantz the CEO didn't know if any scientific evidence existed or not, he was just spit-balling.

He continued: "But we also can't afford to send you to a private hypnotist; we're going to have to make some other sort of arrangement."

"Like what?"

Camus had by this point slumped onto the couch, one hand covering his forehead and eyes, the other holding a scotch. Neither he nor Rosencrantz the CEO knew where the scotch came from, but he wasn't going to complain.

"I'm giving you two tickets to see the Amazing Ralph's show. He's the biggest act in Anytown, USA, which, as you know, is the town wherein this hospital is. My cousin is his manager so I can get a deal on the seats. But you have to promise me you'll volunteer to go on stage to be hypnotized."

"The Amazing Ralph?"

"Yeah. It's only his stage identity—Ralph's not his real name. He's a plumber or something during the day, I think. But you should see his collection of The

Wiggles's memorabilia sometime! The commemorative plates are especially amazing. Some are even autographed! Though not by any of The Wiggles." Rosencrantz the CEO's enthusiasm deflated with this last sentence, replaced by a mild confusion. He was overall having a great time interacting with Camus, but he truly had no sense of irony.

"So let me get this straight—you think I have a terrible anger management problem, so bad that it endangers patients and staff alike, but instead of getting me therapy, you want me to go to a hypnotist performance by the Great—"

"Amazing, not Great. And he's technically a neuroperformanceologist, not a hypnotist," interrupted Rosencrantz the CEO. "And he's also trained in phrenology."

"Okay, I'm going to see the 'Amazing Ralph' the...whatever...to be hypnotized, and then I'm supposed to come back without any anger issues? And I should see his collection of commemorative plates?"

"You'll enjoy it! He goes on right after the ventriloquist. He's very good."

"Who? The ventriloquist or the hypnotist?" Camus asked in perplexed exasperation.

Rosencrantz the CEO wasn't listening closely.

"Yes. Enjoy the show! And come back a changed man so that I don't have to deal with you anymore, hm? And make sure to get some pictures for Ralph. He likes to post things on his Facetwittogram; his adept use of social media looms large in his legend."

"So what if it doesn't work and I remain the charming, superior man that I am now?"

"Then I'll fire you. You're actually not a very good doctor."

Rosencrantz the CEO was bluffing, but Camus really did suck as a physician. He led the staff in malpractice claims, and in Rosencrantz the CEO's mind, that was the crowning characteristic of a terrible physician. Camus was nothing more than an Apple dongle to plug normal headphones into an iPhone— infinitely annoying, more expensive than its worth, already irrelevant because of air pods, and everyone absolutely *despises* the fact that it exists in the first place. But you have to have it to listen to your music. Everyone wanted to sue the hospital simply because Camus the Dongle came into their lives.

"Are you an alcoholic? We have a special deal for our physicians to go to the Jack Daniels Memorial Rehab Center. I hear they let you color during the day for therapy!"

Rosencrantz the CEO was almost considering how to pretend to be an alcoholic to go to the center. They sent so many of their doctors there that if they sent one more, Rosencrantz the CEO could go for free.

"No, I'm not an alcoholic. Rehab will not fix what you think my problem is. Though I hear that coloring can be very helpful. And I know you can't fire me unilaterally. I know how this works," Camus weakly harrumphed, as he didn't have the emotional reserve to yell or curse at this point.

"I guess we'll just have to find out, won't we?"

"This is unbelievable," said Camus defeatedly, though Rosencrantz the CEO thought Camus was impressed with the plan.

"Well, I am kind of without equal," Rosencrantz the CEO said proudly.

Rosencrantz the CEO was convinced that Camus would "fail" his "therapy", so in the meantime he needed to "prep" his "case" to "get rid" of Dr. Camus "completely". Well, completely from the hospital, not to kill him or anything that drastic. The other doctors would just have to pick up the slack for Camus's absence.

"I'm sure they won't mind," Rosencrantz the CEO figured.

He might even get away with not hiring a replacement, even though they were technically understaffed as it was.

"You just need to decide to take the purple pill and accept reality."

"The purple pill is Nexium, not the one that takes you outside the matrix."

While Camus still did not know the correct color of the pill that Lawrence Fishburne's character gave to

Keanu Reeves's, he was confident enough that it wasn't purple. And he was quite pleased with himself for "knowing" that Don Cheadle was the actor, unlike those [BLEEP BLEEP] morons upstairs.

"Ya know, nothing ever changes in this hospital, except for the worse." Camus thought he had hit the coup de grâce.

"Speaking of change, I've been considering changing the hospital's slogan. What do you think of 'We are a hospital—and that's a promise!'" Rosencrantz the CEO was very pleased with himself for this new possibility.

"I don't know. Changing the cadence like that kinda ruins the joke."

Rosencrantz the CEO looked hurt. "Joke? What joke? Our slogan isn't a joke!"

"Really? I always figured we had to have a slogan that stated 'We are a hospital' because the name of this [BLEEP] hospital is too long for anyone to remember. The slogan had to be brief to counteract that. So you're telling me it's a [BLEEP] serious slogan?"

"Yes, of course it is! But don't you think this would be a better slogan?"

"No," replied Camus very matter-of-factly.

"Whatever. Say hi to Ralph for me! Oh, and if you buy his book before the show, you can get it autographed, not by The Wiggles but by him. It's available everywhere books are sold."

Chapter Four
Dr. Camus Might Be a Little Less of a Jerk

"Why in the [BLEEP] world can't I find a parking spot?"

The night was dark, as nights tend to be, and Camus was looking for a parking spot (as per the above dialogue). Tonight was the Amazing Ralph's show.

"Oh no, you've [BLEEP BLEEP] gotta be kidding me."

The strip mall that housed Ralph's show shared a parking lot with an arena. Tonight there was a concert featuring Balsamic Reduction, some stupid trendy band that tweens and teens flocked to.

"Too bad Nickelback isn't playing," thought Camus. They were unironically his favorite band, for no good reason at all.

In Camus's efforts to park, he had to wade through 1) teenage drivers, 2) parents trying to get to the front door to drop off their annoying pre-teen children, and

3) stupid adolescents walking all over the place with no regard for other people, let alone cars.

Camus leaned to the side of his motorcycle as he remained frozen in the traffic.

"Hey, you. Yeah, you [BLEEP BLEEP BLEEP] piece of [BLEEP]. Get out of the way!"

The teenagers receiving Camus's bullying stopped in their tracks with their mouths hanging open; they were so intrigued by his mellifluous cursing artistry that jealousy and awe overcame them. The teenagers did not know what he was asking them to do but were carried off into the moment like a sailor to a Siren's song. They couldn't fully make out his words because the Censor was working tonight, this being an employer-required function, but Camus inspired them nonetheless.

"HEY! I said [BLEEP] with the door handle [BLEEP] fuzzy socks and [BLEEP BLEEP] CLAPPER!" he said with extra emphasis on "clapper", his favorite 1980s invention.

The kids finally snapped back and hurried out of Camus's way. Many of the teenagers trailing behind them, however, continued at their glacial pace.

"I'm never getting through here!"

Camus wanted to use his motorcycle to weave in and out of the cars and crowd, but didn't quite have enough space. He finally just began flooring it on the sidewalk with a primal scream. Though there were some close calls, no one was hurt.

"There, that's more [BLEEP] like it."

Camus was suddenly in a decent mood, though the Censor was a bit out of sorts from the sidewalk driving adventure. He had been riding in the motorcycle's sidecar and was thus in the most danger from Camus's driving antics.

Camus wouldn't admit it to himself, but he was quite intrigued by how the show might go. He hadn't seen a hypnotist since he was in middle school, when his principal went under and clucked like a chicken for all to see. Too bad the hypnotist didn't die in that moment so that the principal would remain in his trance forever.

He walked through the foyer and down the hall towards the auditorium. A dark red flower design that reminded him of a swanky 1970s lounge covered the floor and walls. They did not decorate the building for a kitsch or retro look, however, it simply hadn't been updated for decades. He strolled past the karaoke bar, where a man with a Russian accent was singing a Neil Diamond song. Camus cringed as the singer crooned: "Khello my frend, khello. Just called to let you know, I tsink abowt you evree knite." It somehow didn't quite work. He kept searching for room 101.

"That's a shame about the narrator," mentioned the Censor, making small talk as they walked.

"Why, what happened?"

"She's British. Hence all the big words in her descriptions."

"Oh, that is too bad."

He arrived at the auditorium roughly halfway through the ventriloquist's act. (Slogan: Not just for dummies anymore!) It subconsciously disappointed him that the crowds in the parking lot kept him from arriving on time, but he would never admit that to himself. At least the eleven people present in the 250 seat capacity auditorium seemed to be enjoying themselves.

Camus and the Censor took their seats towards the back of the auditorium. Apprehension accompanied Camus's curiosity; he didn't know what to expect from the Amazing Ralph. Would he still be himself? Would it really improve his anger issues? Or would the hypnotist just embarrass him by making him disco dance? Though Camus convinced himself that he was a great disco dancer. He was not.

A slow trickle of people kept coming in as the ventriloquist completed his act. As you could guess by the very fact that he opened for a hypnotist, he wasn't very good. Many of the people coming in late seemed to understand this, but some of them also seemed to be regulars for the Amazing Ralph. Two ladies in their early twenties even had Ralph tee-shirts on that were obviously homemade. Both the shirts and their large signs that said (creatively enough) "Ralph is AMAZING!" succeeded in having an awful lot of glitter, the excess of which stringed along the floor behind them. They tried to get the growing crowd of about 25 people to chant "Ralph! Ralph! Ralph!" while he was building suspense before coming out for his headlining act. The only person who bought in was an elderly gentleman who was over-exuberant to reconnect, even for a moment, with youthful zeal.

Just then, a voice came over the intercom (that Camus would soon realize was, in fact, Ralph's own voice) introducing the "world famous", "heavily sought after", and many other nondescript lies, "THE. AMAZING. RAAAAAALLLLLLLPPPPPPHHHHHH!"

A portly, bald, and obviously uncomfortable in the spotlight middle-aged hypnotist in a cheap magician's cape appeared from backstage. Even though his beard stubble was the same length as Rosencrantz the CEO's, Ralph's would be described as "unkempt" and "slovenly" compared to the CEO's titillating facial quills.

"Thank you, thank you, I'm glad you're all here," began Ralph, though none of it was believable.

His eyes darted around the room in a suspicious manner, almost like someone who was suspicious and thus looking around the room suspiciously. There were already beads of sweat on his forehead, and the lighting, though incredibly lucent for a small auditorium, made him look a bit pale. Or he was simply incredibly white.

"Let's get right to it. How about some volunteers? I'm gonna need five people to help with this first demonstration."

Camus sank in his seat as nearly everyone in the audience burst out of theirs, eagerly trying to be chosen. The Censor elbowed him.

"The sooner you volunteer, the sooner we can get outta here."

Good point. Camus immediately added his raised arm to the eager crowd. Ralph didn't seem to see him at first, so Camus stood up and began waving his arms.

"Yes, you in the back. Please come up."

Given Ralph's sweat and nervous behavior, Camus wondered if Rosencrantz the CEO had told Ralph ahead of time that Camus was coming.

He had.

"He's probably just in awe of me," thought Camus.

He wasn't.

The Censor, though having had no medical training whatsoever, aside from the thousands of hours spent shadowing Camus, had other suspicions of what could cause Ralph's currently apparent distress.

"Please, each of you sit right here," Ralph instructed.

The elderly man enthralled with the young women joined them and Camus on stage. Ralph neglected to select a fifth volunteer; he wasn't feeling well and just wanted to get the show over with. His mild difficulty in breathing was becoming more apparent.

Despite this, Ralph wanted to try something new.

"Instead of putting all of you under at the same time, I would like to try this one at a time so that we can explore some unique things with each person."

By "unique things", he really meant "even more embarrassing." Though the weight of having to cure Dr. Camus of all of his weaknesses sat heavy on Ralph, he wanted to debase Camus for a while first.

"Let's start with this gentleman here," Ralph said as he motioned to Dr. Camus.

The crowd let out a sigh of disappointment, as there was a large contingent present to enjoy the hypnotism of the two young sycophants.

Ralph was wiping his sweat nearly constantly. He wasn't sure what was happening, as this wasn't a typical thing for him. He had never been this anxious for a show, and he felt so out of sorts that he even forgot to warn the crowd not to try all of this at home, that he was a trained professional, and that they could cause others some severe harm blah blah blah. There were multiple pre-teen boys in the audience paying close attention so that they could cause such harm to their younger brothers that night.

"Watch this pocket watch, and follow it with your eyes, back and forth, back and forth. I am going to count down from five, and then snap my fingers. When you hear that snap, you will go into a trance, a hypnotic state, and you will be forced to obey all of my commands. You will not awake until you hear the key word: boondoggle. 5...4...3...2...1...snap!"

It worked. Camus, cynical to the very end, felt all conscious thought leave his head, though he wasn't quite conscious of it actually happening. His head fell down, and he felt as though he was stuck in a hollowed out tunnel of thick cheese. Probably cheddar, though it could be American, he wasn't quite sure. He could still hear Ralph, but faintly and muffled, the neuroperformanceologist's voice sounding like Charlie Brown's school teacher. Camus came out the other side of the cheese to a sense of pure calm, almost Zen-like in its simplicity and profoundness. He was swimming in the ocean, staring up at a beautiful, starry sky. His heart slowed to a steady beat. Every skin cell on his body felt the cool water, a perfectly mindful state. He carried no guile for anyone or anything. Everything inside him melted into a pure oblivion of bliss.

And then he was clucking like a chicken.

He couldn't help it. As he danced across the stage, he was flapping his arms up and down like he was flying. He wasn't sure why he was doing it; it was as if he had no control over himself. Though he didn't really mind. It was almost liberating, the ability to act like a fool yet not even consciously realize that is what he was doing. He somehow knew that his subconscious had taken over, but it felt so amazing that he fully embraced it. He was free from himself. After a few minutes, his time as a chicken abruptly ended at Ralph's command.

Suddenly, as we foreshadowed many-a-time in this story, and a trope so common we could not possibly leave it out of this tale, the Amazing Ralph collapsed. Everyone ran over to him, except for the one doctor in the room who was still swimming in the ocean of complacency. Ralph wasn't breathing. He was completely pale. A middle-aged woman from the audience began performing CPR, something she learned by watching lots of medical procedurals on TV. But as one would expect from such an education, she didn't do it correctly, her elbows flapping open in her compressions, which thus provided no compression at all. To give chest compressions correctly, the chest needs to be compacted two-to-three inches, a depth which is more likely than not to break some ribs. I'm sure dead Ralph would be grateful that his ribs were intact, however.

He never woke up. The ambulance arrived about 30 minutes later, but their efforts at resuscitation were also useless. (They would have been there sooner, but another ambulance crew had poured sugar in their gas tank as a prank, so they had to spend a few extra minutes locating a functioning ambulance, and then wade through the concert crowd in the parking lot.) They pronounced the Amazing Ralph dead at 8:43, about 35 minutes after Dr. Camus was hypnotized. And hypnotized, he would remain.

Chapter Five
Dr. Camus is Not a Jerk?

Camus awoke the next morning as refreshed and buoyant as ever before. He couldn't remember any details of the night before, though he remembered how it felt. He honestly thought that the Censor had slipped him some acid.

"I haven't had LSD in years!" he said to himself, mostly because there wasn't anyone else there to say it to. "This is great!"

He immediately called the Censor to get his take on the evening.

"Hi, this is Blaine."

"Censor? Is that you? How come I never knew your name was Blaine? This is a complete revelation to me!"

"Uh oh," thought Blaine the Censor. He had tried to keep his name secret for years because he knew the impending and never-ending scorn and ridicule he would endure for the rest of his professional life with Dr. Camus.

"Uh, yeah, that's my name," he grimaced.

"Wow, I never would have guessed. You don't look like a Blaine. Anyway, what happened last night?"

Blaine was amazed—no jokes at his expense? No condescension or lampooning of his name? He had been ashamed of his name since childhood, given his constant ridicule. Probably because it was a simply terrible name to have.

"Camus must just be keeping me in suspense until he rains down the ridicule," he thought.

But then Blaine had another thought—Dr. Camus had already spoken multiple sentences with no obscenities. Blaine always knew when they were coming, but his spidey-sense hadn't yet tingled at all.

"Something's wrong," he thought.

"What foulness has become you?" asked Blaine.

"'What foulness has become me?' Why are you talking like that? Who are you, Dr. Doff?"

"Sorry, I've been prepping for a Renaissance fair coming up."

Blaine the Censor immediately winced at revealing yet another embarrassing fact about himself to Camus.

"Well, you still need to practice. You should say 'what foulness has become thee?' instead of 'you.'"

Okay, something really *was* wrong.

"Camus, I think we need to take you to the hospital."

"Good idea. I have to get reinstated by Mr. Rosencrantz the CEO."

Calling the CEO "Mr. Rosencrantz the CEO" was the last straw.

"No, I actually mean to the emergency room."

"You mean 'emergency department'. Don't say 'emergency room' or they'll kick you out," Camus said with a twinkle in his eye. Alas, there were no emergency room, er, sorry, emergency *department* staff around to thank him for the distinction.

"Why are you so concerned, anyway?" queried Camus.

"You're not acting like yourself. You're not mocking me, you're not cursing, and you're referring to the hospital CEO respectfully. Something's wrong."

"Hey, I just feel good today. It is what it is."

Blaine demurred: "No, it *isn't* 'what it is'. It's actually something completely different. It's what it *isn't*. I didn't know that was possible until now, but here we are."

"Well, either way, I'm not going to the ED. You wanna come with me to see Mr. Rosencrantz the CEO?"

"I suppose I better. Maybe seeing him will put you back in your foul, cursing mood. Just let me put in some dry shampoo first." *NAAAHHHH!* Blaine inaudibly screamed to himself.

This was not his day.

. . .

"I'm sorry Dr. Camus, Mr. Rosencrantz the CEO is in a meeting," said the administrative assistant politely, though inside he was bracing for a verbal berating.

"Okay, I know he's a busy man. I'll wait right here."

Both Chad the Administrative Assistant and Blaine glanced sideways at Camus. Why wasn't he upset about waiting? Why didn't he storm into the meeting? And why was Chad even polite to him in the first place? Shouldn't he return the scorn which he had repeatedly received from Camus over the years? Chad the Administrative Assistant should have kicked Camus in the shin the moment he saw him coming, but now almost felt bad about it. The near-guilt quickly passed.

"Dr. Camus, are you alright today?" asked Chad the Administrative Assistant in a very administrative assistant-like way.

"Yes, fine. Thank you for asking. And you?"

"Just feeling a bit off, maybe from the full moon we had last night. There was also an entire group of dogs endlessly howling all night, so I didn't sleep well. I'm not sure why they howled so much more last night than at other full moons."

Camus smiled at him, not sure what to say. The boardroom door burst open, saving Camus some awkwardness with Chad the Administrative Assistant, and a roar of laughter and back slapping emerged ahead of Rosencrantz the CEO.

"And I'm sure that means we'll *all* be dead soon!" Rosencrantz the CEO said to a woman at his side as they heartily chortled.

Rosencrantz the CEO greeted everyone as they left the board meeting, each of them wearing their brash, overpriced clothes, and headed to their lush BMW's and Jaguar's. As the last person exited, Rosencrantz the CEO froze with eyes wide when he saw Camus in the waiting room.

"You're not supposed to be here! What are you doing? What happened with Ralph?" he asked rhetorically in fear, as he sputtered back into the boardroom for safety.

"It's okay. I know you're busy. We'll just wait here until you're available," Camus yelled into the room.

Rosencrantz the CEO needed time to process. What was going on? He wasn't supposed to see Camus for a month. Did he have any legal recourse against Camus being here? Couldn't he call security and have Camus escorted out of the building? It was only a suspension. That didn't mean he couldn't come on the premises, did it? Rosencrantz the CEO backed into the corner of the room, a puddle of sweat forming in his Italian silk suit, and waited for Camus to enter and rip him apart. He couldn't help but let out a very high-pitched scream.

"Are you okay, sir?" asked Chad the Administrative Assistant as he looked into the room—now empty of all but Rosencrantz the CEO.

"Yeah, yeah, I'm fine," he answered unconvincingly. "That sound was probably just the hospital settling."

"Shall I get you your typical tea and mayonnaise?"

"Um, yes, that would be good."

Rosencrantz the CEO immediately felt a little better.

Camus figured this was as good a time as any to talk with him.

"Since everyone has left the meeting, is this a good time to chat for a minute?"

Suddenly Camus's behavior dawned on Rosencrantz the CEO.

"Wait, why are you being polite? And not cursing? Are you trying to set me up? Is this some kind of trick?"

"Not at all. I feel like I've had a lot of things clear up for me recently and I'd like to come back to work."

"Are you saying that the Amazing Ralph actually helped?"

Rosencrantz the CEO visibly brightened but remained in the corner in case Camus's behavior suddenly turned vile.

"I don't know, but it appears that he died last night."

"Not Ralph?! That's terrible. What happened?"

"He collapsed after putting me under. I don't know all the details, but it didn't appear they could revive him. I was too busy swimming in the ocean."

"Did you at least get a picture with Ralph? Or see his Wiggles collection?"

"I unfortunately did not have the pleasure."

Rosencrantz the CEO instantly realized what was happening with Camus. (Being an amoral administrator and a moron didn't keep him from seeing the obvious, at least in this case.)

"So you're not angry? Or mean? How do I know you're not lying?"

"All I can say is that I seem to view life in a new way," Camus chuckled amiably.

Rosencrantz the CEO cocked an eyebrow.

"Do you even remember what you're like? Do you remember how terrible of a person you are? How much you hate me and I hate you?"

"Kind of. I know that I've been terrible, and I'm sorry for that. It's like the memory of a dream that's on the tip of your tongue, but you just can't quite remember it. It's all there, but it's as though my subconscious has overtaken my previous conscious choices.

"I think it may have even unlocked some repressed memories. I've been having some very vivid thoughts about aliens examining me since last night."

"Censor, what do you think?" Rosencrantz the CEO wasn't sure what he was supposed to do.

"I don't know. I guess it's possible that the hypnotism unlocked some repressed memories. It used to be done often, and more people likely were abducted than we know about."

"No, you idiot, about what we should do with our little Dr. Camus here." Rosencrantz the CEO was a bit flustered, though strangely curious to hear more about the aliens.

"He must have hit his head or something. He might need a cat scan," said Blaine.

"Well, it was a full moon last night. But despite the hypnotism, and the vernal equinox tomorrow, and all the howling dogs, and the pagans that have been doing some weird rituals across the street for the last week, it's probably just a coincidence. Or maybe deep down, you *are* a decent guy and Ralph just unleashed it. Remember, you *are* the Chosen one." But Rosencrantz the CEO couldn't quite accept that.

"Nope. Again, you're thinking of Phil."

"I don't know why I can't remember that. Have you met his new wife? She's so great."

"Yeah, you've mentioned her before, the fundraising. She sounds swell. But my change is just one of those things," mused Camus.

"'Those things' don't exist. Something covered up your typical...how shall I say this?...Brutish personality." Coming up with euphemisms was not one of Blaine's strong suits, but he was feeling very nervous that his job could be in trouble if Camus kept his language clean.

"Well, you can't come back early, if that's what you want. I've already added your month's salary back into the budget."

Rosencrantz the CEO didn't dare tell Camus that it was for new furniture in his own office.

"That's fine. I'll do it without pay."

Rosencrantz the CEO's eyes lit up. A doctor working for free? Was that even possible?! If Camus set this precedent, there's no end to how much money Rosencrantz the CEO could tussle away from his medical staff. He wasn't sure if the legal department could undo the suspension, but this was too good of an opportunity to pass up. He could convince the hospital's Department of Legal-Type Things and How to Get Away with Stuff to come up with *some* way out of it.

"Okay Camus, have it your way. You can come back immediately without pay for one month. But if you are back to *any* of your old shenanigans, I'll suspend you for another month without pay. You really should be more like Phil. And his wife." No one was sure what the deal was with Rosencrantz the CEO and Phil's wife, but it was getting a little creepy.

"Ya know, it's almost as though I forgot that practicing medicine is all about—"

Camus's musing was cut off by Rosencrantz the CEO.

"—the private insurance? I know what you mean."

"Well, I was going to say *the patients*, but I suppose it is important to make some money for the hospital, too."

Rosencrantz the CEO scowled in horror at Camus's uncharacteristic comment. "Anywhoo, let's go see what The Don has to say about this."

• • •

Camus, Blaine, and Rosencrantz the CEO found Dr. Doff strolling through the small flower garden just outside of the Labor and Delivery Unit. He seemed literally to be smelling the (dying) roses, eyes closed, an air of satisfaction on his face, while his hands held each other behind his back, as if he had not a care in the world. A smothered rose bush remained flattened from the drunk man Camus unloaded from the ED just yesterday.

The garden was relatively new, the brain-child of Rosencrantz the CEO. There weren't very many babies being born at The Amicus Health Priority Catalyst Wellness Code Blue Peloton Forward Crescendo Care Memorial Hospital of Her Motherly Excellence for a while. Most of the local doctors refused to have their patients sent there, as the unit was under-staffed and poorly equipped to handle deliveries. The frequent changing of the guard of traveling nurses led to potential delivery complications, as the staff rarely knew where anything was. All the expectant mothers were thus going to the Good Hospital not far up the road.

In order to rectify the situation, Rosencrantz the CEO decided that more business would come if the hospital grounds were a bit more beautiful. A nice flower garden outside the windows of the patient's rooms is what would lead to better business, er, patient care. They quickly planted the flowers and expected the insurance money from healthy mothers with healthy babies to come rolling in. But it never happened. It turns out that nice flowers don't make a lick of difference in having a healthy, well-attended mother and baby. Besides, in order to even see the flowers, the shades had to be up in the patient's room, so any passer-by could see the mother laboring, or breastfeeding, or cleaning up the blood and other fluids that naturally accompany birth.

At least it was better than his other idea to increase business. Rosencrantz the CEO thought they could put a sign with a QR code outside the hospital. Anyone who opened the link through their phone would literally become afflicted with a "fun" mystery disease that the hospital's doctors would then have a contest to see who could diagnose the fastest. The treatment would still cost, though. Alas, the technology isn't that far advanced yet.

"Hey guys. What's up?" Dr. Doff offered up when he heard the three men coming.

"Wait, why are you talking like that? You never talk like that. What's going on? Are you feeling okay? Are you sick or something?" Camus asked, confusingly.

Doff wasn't speaking in his typical high-brow WASP-y way. Saying "What's up?" isn't exactly the same as his usual "How dost thou, honourable gentlemen?"

"What do you mean? This is just how I talk. I'm actually feeling pretty fantastic, thanks dude."

Rosencrantz the CEO didn't care how Doff was talking, but wanted him to shut up because he never much liked what Doff had to say regardless of how he said it.

"Hmm, fine. Well, Doffy, it appears that our Dr. Camus is healed of his wretched ways and will be coming back to the hospital immediately."

"Great news! But don't let me hear that you're up to your old shenanigans again. Those Orthopedic Surgeons and Dr. Reg really have it in for you now, and I don't blame them at all. Otherwise, I don't really care what happens."

Not only was Doff speaking differently than he typically did, but he didn't seem to have his usual avuncular nature—he appeared detached. Camus always thought that Doff had his back. Maybe he only did it to keep Camus from bothering him even more. More importantly, only Blaine seemed a little confused as to the over-use of the word "shenanigans" by professionals.

"Great chat. I'll head up to the medical floor right now."

Camus was ready to go.

Chapter Six
Dr. Camus is a Somewhat Decent Guy that is Not a Jerk

"Where did all these staff come from? I've never seen half of these people. There are so many nurses, and doctors, and aides—I only remember seeing a few at a time. And when did they hire so many female physicians? They're everywhere!"

Camus couldn't believe the hustle occurring around the nurse's station upstairs.

"Geez, Ralph really *did* do a number on you," Blaine answered. "They've always been here, at The Motherly Excellence Peloton Forward Crescendo Care Amicus Health Priority Catalyst Wellness Blue Code Memorial Hospital. You probably were too much in your own narcissistic world to notice them all, Jacksonian."

Uh oh. Blaine didn't mean to call Camus by his first name. Fireworks would inevitably ensue. But Camus hardly noticed.

"Hi everybody! I'm baaa-aaaaack!" Camus said in a loud, non-*Poltergeist*-like voice.

They only suspended him yesterday, but in his mind, it felt like weeks. Nobody replied, aside from a few grunts.

"Does nobody care that I'm here?" Camus asked Blaine.

"Yes. I mean no. I don't know what the correct way to answer that is except to say that you are correct—nobody likes you. Sometimes they egg you on to get you upset and enjoy a show, but mostly they just ignore you."

"Blanche! Blanche, is that you? It's me, Dr. Camus!" he called down the hall towards the new nurse whom he harangued only the day before.

Blaine thought she had quit on the spot, but it turned out that she came back once she heard of Camus's suspension. Her dark eyes widened with terror and confusion, and she took off running.

"No, wait! Blanche, I want to apologize! I know it's rough starting a new job, especially your first job out of school, and I messed it up for you. I'm sorry!"

Everyone stopped in their tracks when they heard Camus's apology being yelled down the hallway. Jaws dropped. Hearts skipped a beat. Nobody even noticed the psychiatric patient slip out the door to horrible freedom. No one spoke until Blanche started screaming. She screamed so loud it echoed in the stairwell and travelled down the hall. Everyone rushed to the windows to watch as she left the building and ran out into traffic, only narrowly avoiding serious injury.

Back at the nurses' station, some wanted to, but didn't dare, ask why Camus was acting so strange.

"Look, I know what you're all thinking," Camus began.

Except that most of them were inexplicably thinking about the pros and cons of the economic arbitrage pricing theory versus the capital asset pricing model, so Camus really did not know what they were thinking at all.

"Something's happened to me, and I just see things a little differently now."

"Did you get, like, new glasses or something?" someone asked in the back of the crowd.

Considering that Camus didn't wear glasses, he ignored the comment.

"I'm just...I'm just...I'm just sorry to all of you."

"Gasp!" said the crowd altogether.

"I fully intend to make it up to you, or my name isn't Jacksonian Democracy Camus!"

Everyone was confused. Was he saying that *was* his name, or was *not* his name? It was a weird name, they all thought in unison, but weird enough that he shouldn't need to state that it *wasn't* his name. Though it would explain a lot if that *was* his name. Was it a joke? What if he was just messing with them?

One staff whispered to the nurse next to them, "What does 'Jacksonian Democracy' mean?" The nurse, with a blank face and eyes full of confusion, slowly pointed to Camus.

"So..." the unit's administrator cleared their throat, "...Dr. Jacksonian...uh...Democracy Camus, is your suspension over?"

"No. Well, yes. Well, I guess, it's kind of—I don't know. Think of this as, like, the obsessive Indian-meditation, one-with-all-living-things, phase of my career."

"Wait, you're going to India?! And since when were you into meditation? 'One-with-all-living-things'?! What does all this have to do with you coming back to the hospital?" confusingly asked Nurse Man.

"What? No, I'm not going to India. I'm obviously not explaining this very well. Blaine, you tell them."

"Dr. Camus is allowed to see patients, effective immediately."

"Good. Your three patients with pneumonoultra... whatever are all still here, and *not* responding to your 'usual treatment,'" said Nurse Man.

Nurse Man, whose name Camus now learned was Dennis, smirked with satisfaction. Despite sharing a beer the day before, Dennis still detested Camus.

"Schnookerdookies! I guess I'll have to re-assess their diagnosis."

Blaine was ready to BLEEP Camus, but had to catch himself since Camus didn't actually curse. Blaine's eyes widened; suddenly, he *knew* that his entire livelihood was at serious risk.

Chapter Seven
Dr. Camus is Not Insulting in this Chapter

Dr. Camus was once again finding his footing as a physician, but more the physician he initially started out as. He had only been back at the hospital for a few days, but was hitting his stride, or finding his groove, or hitting his groove, or even finding his stride, I'm not sure which. He almost enjoyed being a doctor again.

"Dr. Camus! Dr. Camus! We need your help! Can you come assist us in the clinic for a few hours? Everyone called in sick today to go skiing."

It didn't matter that Camus was a hospitalist. Anyone can do outpatient medicine, right? Right?! (The answer is no.)

"Sure, I'd be happy to help," Dr. Camus responded to the pleasant medical assistant.

It is now the time where we cue the montage of Dr. Camus seeing patients that are all really stupid and we watch his dumbfounded responses. Below are merely the highlights:

"Well Mr., uh..." Camus cleared his throat, "...Thompson. I think I found your diagnosis—you're actually a woman."

• • •

"Dr. Camel, I just, I don't know, Dr. Camel. You know how, like, stuff just *happens*, Dr. Camel? You know how things happen, right? I mean, I don't, I don't, like, I don't know how I could have gotten pregnant, Dr. Camel. I mean, I didn't swim in the that lake by my house like my boyfriend said. I didn't go back to the, like, to the palm reader that my boyfriend told me to stay away from, Dr. Camel. And I used exactly the type of, like, pen that he said I should use to keep from getting pregnant, Dr. Camel. These things were supposed to keep me from, like, getting pregnant, ya know? Ya know, Dr. Camel?"

• • •

"Dude, like all I did was flip my hair to get it out of my eyes, and now my neck is killing me! I probably broke something, don't ya think?"

"My other doctor told me that to fix my diabetes, I would need to decrease the sugars that I eat. So now I've gone on an all pasta-diet and my diabetes is even worse!"

. . .

"I got all of these scrapes on my back from riding my hoverboard. I fell off, but my shoelaces were stuck in it, and it somehow kept going. It dragged me halfway down the block before my brother caught up to me and stopped it. I need you to make it sound really serious so that I can sue them."

"But you're only thirteen!" said Camus in dismay.

"A girl's gotta start somewhere. You think I should sue the shoelace company, too?"

. . .

"How did your eyes get so red, sir?" Camus asked.

"I got dem dare hiccups. It mades me so sore that I couldn't'a get rid a 'em. I grabbed my 'Off' bug spree and spreed me whole fece. It sure done stopped dem hiccups, k'sept now I cern't see. It mait be reactin' wit da chip da governmnt put in me frum da covid shot."

. . .

"Doctor, I need you to check out my elderly father. His bowel movements have become churlish and counterfeit."

. . .

"I asked my sister who works at the front desk of the hospital why I was feeling this way, and she said it might be a stroke. So I looked up my symptoms on the internet and it said I could have cancer. I'm going to need a MRI of my brain, all of my vitamin levels checked, and a full genetic workup."

"What were your symptoms?"

"My toe hurt."

"I see."

"It's fine now, though."

. . .

"Oh man, I can't believe this happened to me. Oh! I was singing with my band Balsamic Reduction at this rockin' new venue, right? I went to slide across the stage on my, my, ya know, my knees, right? But I guess that leather pants don't slide very well on sticky floors. Amiright? And so my knees just stopped, and my head kept going, right into the stage. And since then I've been confused with a headache, vomiting, and I've got this big gash on my forehead. Pretty rock 'n roll, right?! I guess I lost that bet."

"I have an irrational fear that I am being watched in my sleep by a man in a carrot costume."

"And what would you like me to do about that?" asked Dr. Camus while he scratched his forehead in the disbelief that this was really happening to him.

"I want you to kill him."

By this point of the day, Camus couldn't even muster surprise.

• • •

As Dr. Camus exited the clinic in a daze from his patient encounters, the medical assistant asked, "Dr. Camus? Why aren't you in some nice outpatient clinic instead of working in that terrible hospital?"

"Frankly, outpatient clinics don't make for a continuously interesting story. People prefer the acuity that's in a hospital setting. Every medical drama or comedy or dramedy takes place in the hospital, not a clinic or a nursing home or...or...someplace else. Can I have some ibuprofen, please?"

The assistant didn't understand what Camus was talking about, and so figured that he needed the ibuprofen all the more.

• • •

"Dr. Camus! Dr. Camus! We need your help in the ED, stat!"

"How do all these people know my name? I don't remember any of them," Camus thought to himself. "What is it?" Camus asked the person cautiously.

"The emergency department. You know, the ED. Where sick and injured people go for emergency health care?" She was obviously new.

"Yes, I know what the ED is. *What is it you need me to do?*"

"We just got a whole car full of clowns with glitter lung! A glitter cannon accidentally went off in the car and there are about thirty clowns now who can't breathe!"

"Hmm. Well, I can honestly say I've never seen *this* before," Camus mused to himself as he rushed to the ED.

.

"Dr. Camus! Dr. Camus! We need your help!" Camus wasn't sure who that was or what needed help, but he was willing to try despite his crazy afternoon in the clinic and the ED.

"What is it?" he asked worriedly.

"You know, 'help', like when you provide someone needed assistance?"

He was obviously new.

"Okay, what 'help' do you need?" answered Camus as patiently as possible.

"We need you to perform an autopsy, stat!"

Dr. Camus gave his patented (it wasn't really patented) dumbfounded look with a mild recoil of his head. This request irked him.

"First of all, I'm not a pathologist, so why in the world would I be performing an autopsy? Second, since when does an autopsy need to be done stat?"

"Mr. Rosencrantz the CEO said something about getting sued if we don't do it NOW, and you're the only doctor in the hospital."

"Seriously? *Everyone* else went skiing?" Camus grumbled as he headed down the stairs to the morgue.

"Look, I'm still ten feet away and I can tell exactly what killed him!" Camus started when he saw the body, though it was really about twelve feet, not ten. "He has a harpoon in his chest! Why do we need a frickin' autopsy?!"

Yes, in his frustration, he actually said "frickin". He was starting to lose it.

"Evidently the man's wife is gonna sue us if we don't confirm the actual cause of death. Even though she saw the whole thing happen, she doesn't *actually* believe that harpoons can kill someone. She said she saw something about it on Fox News."

"So, do I have to find some other cause of death? I guess I'll just put in the report that he had a sudden-onset cardiovascular collapse. Then she'll have something she can tell her kids to get genetic testing for.

"Too bad he died wearing dirty underwear; my mother always warned me about that."

Camus completed the report in barely under three hours.

• • •

"Dr. Camus! Dr. Camus! We need your help in the OR, stat!" someone ran towards him, yelling.

"No! I don't do surgery."

"Oh." The nurse, crestfallen, walked slowly back into the OR to the sound of a cardiac flatline. Thankfully, it was actually the sound of the hospital's dial-up internet reconnecting, but she didn't yet know that.

Chapter Eight
Dr. Camus is a Nice Guy?

"Okay Ms. Smith, I—" Camus began, but she cut him off immediately.

"Your hands are freezing! Stop touching me. And you don't look like a doctor. Are you sure you really are one? And where is my breakfast?! You people are keeping me here against my will and I won't stand for it!"

Ms. Smith had been cranky her whole life, but now she wasn't thinking clearly because of her pneumonoultramicro...oh wait, I mean pneumonia.

"We're doing the best we can. We've got you on some good medications, and I'll make sure the kitchen delivers your food as soon as possible. Okay?"

Camus was trying to be patient, but he was hitting his limits.

"You better! My neighbor is the CEO of this place, so I can call him at the drop of a hat and get you fired!"

Considering her delirium, Camus didn't know if her threat was real or not. Regardless, he snapped.

"You know what? You do that! It doesn't bother me one bit!" and stormed out of the room.

It had been nearly two weeks since he came back to work, and his newfound optimism was quickly fading. He tried to calm himself as he stood at the nurse's station in the hall, but he was having a hard time. Ms. Smith was getting to him, as were many other patients he'd seen today. The patients were piling up in the ED again for admission, adding to the immense stress of caring for all the patients he already had. He still had a dozen or so notes to write and a bunch of tests to follow up on. Why did he come back early? Maybe he should have stayed home awhile.

"So which antidepressant are you on?" a vaguely familiar voice asked Camus as he leaned on the counter at the nurse's station, head in his hands.

"What?" he said, as he looked up in annoyance.

He saw Dr. Sapient, the very competent and direct orthopedic surgeon who had embarrassed him earlier in this story, with a very matter of fact look on her face.

"Every doctor is on one at some point, and that is really the only explanation for your improved behavior recently. So which is it? I favor sertraline, but I know others prefer different ones."

"No...no, I'm not on any medication. I'm just...I don't know...there was a full moon, and pagans, and a hypnotist, and then the dogs, and now I'm like this. Ugh! And I have a bad headache. It's actually quite hard to be a doctor when you're really trying, you know?"

"Yeah, I get it," Sapient replied with a mild disappointment that he wasn't on medication. "You really are a cliché, aren't you?"

"So I hear. Now I remember why you always propelled me," Camus responded.

Sapient gave a significantly confused look. This is the part where, if the Censor were present, he would tell Camus that what he meant was 'repelled' instead of 'propelled'. But he wasn't here, so Camus had to dangle on the vine of his befuddling comment alone.

Before Camus even recognized Sapient's confusion, their captivating conversation was interrupted.

"Hey Dr. Camus, how's it goin'? Have you considered my proposal any further?"

The orderly seemed slightly over-excited and nervous as she asked what he thought of her proposed business venture.

"Oh, and hi Dr. Sapient," Julie the Orderly said with something of a glower.

There's a long backstory why Julie hates Dr. Sapient, but we won't get into that now, as it doesn't seem fully relevant to the current story. Yet one more exciting reason to await the prequel!

"Julie, I don't know. A café in a barbershop? That actually seems pretty gross. All the hair trimmings will get in your food, and it seems like two things that shouldn't go together. I'm sorry, but I'm not going to invest. Forgive me."

Dr. Camus seemed genuinely sorry for this, but it really was a stupid idea.

"Wow, you *are* just a cliché like everyone says," Julie the Orderly retorted.

"Why does everybody keep saying that?" Camus mumbled to himself.

"Why don't you stick with your idea from a few years ago of a wheelchair with bicycle pedals?" Dr. Sapient said with a sneer worthy of Caligula. (I guess we don't know for sure if Caligula sneered a lot, but he seems like the type, don't you think?)

"Hey, that was a good idea! Someday I'll get people to support my ideas, you'll see!"

"But if someone needs a wheelchair, why would they have bicycle pedals? They won't be able to use them! They're in a wheelchair!" Dr. Sapient couldn't help herself, and was thoroughly enjoying getting her digs in at Julie. You can probably begin to see what some of their backstory may be....

"And what about the '5k to Support Cancer'?"

"We need to raise money to fight cancer. What is wrong with you?" answered Julie.

"You can't call a charity event '*to Support* Cancer', you ding-dong! It sounds like you are trying to give everyone the disease!"

Julie instantly recognized that Sapient had a point, but she wouldn't give Sapient the credit.

"Or your idea for cereal made of jawbreakers? What about your scratch-and-sniff cards to help you identify different smelling animal feces? Or drive-by autopsies?" Sapient jabbed.

"But that's not fair! You can't attack every idea someone has! You need to brainstorm with people to sort it all out!" Julie was nearly in tears.

"Wait, what?"

Karen the Nurse butted in right at this moment, wanting the complete history of the last three minutes and everything that was said. Everyone groaned.

"You can't enter a conversation near the end and expect to be brought up to speed! That's not how this works!" Sapient, Camus, and Julie all said in startling unison.

"Fine. See if I care," Karen said as she stormed off.

"Did you know she's related to The Captain?" Camus asked Sapient.

"Who? What captain? What are you talking about?"

"Never mind."

"I heard you lost a patient yesterday," Camus stated to Sapient with sincere compassion.

Her eyes darkened a bit. "Yeah, a terrible case of migratory hallitosis. It was too late. There wasn't much we could do."

"That's awful, I'm sorry. That's the second time that diagnosis has come up in this story. I never knew it could be deadly."

"No, it killed the nurse, not the patient. The smell was too much. We just ended up sending the patient to the rehab center early."

Camus seemed somewhat impressed by this.

"Are you religious? That seems to help a lot of people during such hard times."

"Yeah, I'm a pescatarian," answered Dr. Sapient.

"Hmm, that seems to be growing in popularity," said Camus confusedly. "Ya know, I think I've recently come to realize that a doctor's job isn't to defeat death, but merely to confuse it for a while."

Sapient seemed genuinely moved by Camus's wisdom.

"That's pretty good. How did you come up with that?"

"It was in my fortune cookie," Camus said with no trace of irony.

"Nice. Even if we only get to 'confuse death' for a time, it's still pretty cool to be a doctor, right?" reflected Sapient.

"I guess. I know that we're revered in society and whatnot, but little do people know that all of those years of schooling, long shifts, and killing ourselves to attain such a prestigious profession really just buys us the luxury of getting other people's poop on ourselves every day. It's kinda gross being a doctor."

Camus thought this was quite profound.

"Yeah, I guess. Hey, where's the Censor? I haven't seen him in a few days."

"Yeah, there isn't much of a need for him any longer, since I'm not a cursing creep anymore. He's trying to find a new job so that he doesn't lose his boat and second house."

Camus seemed genuinely distraught over this, as well; he simply wasn't the man he used to be.

"Camus! What have you been doing?!" Rosencrantz the CEO yelled as he walked down the hall towards the nurse's station.

"What? I didn't do anything!"

"Then who is constantly doing that Mongolian throat singing crap just outside of the C-suites? You're making me regret bringing you back."

"What? Mongolian throat singing...? Oh, you probably mean Dennis the Nurse Man. That's not throat singing, he's practicing to set the world record for gurgling the longest. Did you know it's like seventeen minutes or something? Isn't that incredible? He does it by you guys so that he doesn't bother the patients."

"'Gurgling'? Don't you mean 'gargling'?" Rosencrantz the CEO was confused for more than one reason.

"Oh, yeah, ha, I guess I do."

"Well, I don't want to hear it any longer. Tell him to do it anywhere else."

Rosencrantz the CEO stormed off.

"Hey Lenny?" Camus yelled down the hall in Rosencrantz the CEO's direction.

Rosencrantz the CEO stopped in his tracks while everyone around simultaneously pulled an "Oooooohhhhh."

"What did you call me, Jacksonian?"

Camus was confused.

"Lenny. That's your name, right? I figured we had improved to the point where we could call each other by our first names."

"Nobody, but NOBODY, calls me Lenny except my mother. GOT IT?!"

"Why is that phrase 'nobody but nobody'? That never made much sense to me. Why the 'but'?" Camus sincerely asked no one in particular but everyone in attendance.

"Why the 'but' indeed," responded Lenny...er...Rosencrantz the CEO, as he slowly backed away. He continued staring Camus in the eyes while slowly nodding his head. "Why the 'but', indeed."

"Okay, what just happened?" Camus asked, looking around after Rosencrantz the CEO left.

"I think Rosencrantz the CEO liked you better when you were a jerk," Sapient said with a smirk.

Just then, they heard nondescript yelling coming from the stairwell.

"What was that?" asked Sapient.

"Might be Dennis again," mused Camus. "Or possibly the hospital settling. That seems to happen a lot, these days."

Emerging from the bursting open door came a not-quite-human form with ripped scrubs, a prominent limp, and tousled hair. The emerging gremlin wore a confused and frightened look on its face. There was also what appeared to be car oil smeared all over.

"What the..." said Julie.

Coming slowly down the hall, with the entire staff watching on, crept the medical student, two weeks after running away from embarrassing himself with his unintentional-yet-extremely problematic statements on race during the discussion of the pill's actual colors in the first chapter.

"What happened to you?" Camus asked imploringly. "We haven't seen you since the first chapter."

"I...I...got lost in the basement. Have you...have you ever been down there? It's terrifying. TERRIFYING, I tell you! Dead bodies...rats...ghosts...rats...dead bodies...the cafeteria. You can't believe how many used bed pans are down there! There's gotta be a thousand of them! I didn't know what to do."

He still had a crazed look in his eyes and seemed not to look at any person specifically but through them to the ether beyond.

"Don't you know the areas on the map yet? The directory maps are posted everywhere. Why didn't you just go to Area 50 by the elevators and ask someone for help? Don't they still go over that in orientation?" quipped Sapient with disdain.

"I'm a student...People get mad when you...when you...when you ask too many questions."

He had a point.

"Wait, isn't it 51?" Camus asked sincerely.

"51? What do you mean?" Sapient responded, looking askance at Camus.

"I think that spot on the building directory is Area 51, not 50."

The medical student seemed about to explode in sheer terror and confusion. "AREA 51?! THERE ARE ALIENS DOWN THERE, TOO? This hospital is a nightmare. I thought I was learning to become a doctor, not being sucked into a galactic vortex!"

Everyone looked at the student in curious confusion.

"Were the aliens white?" threw out an orderly, not-so-gently ribbing the student.

"LOOK! I DROPPED MY PAGER IN THE TOILET AND COULDN'T THINK STRAIGHT! I THOUGHT I WOULD GET KICKED OUT OF SCHOOL! IT'S

THAT SIMPLE! STOP LOOKING AT ME LIKE I'M NUTS!"

No one could quite grasp how a medical student could get lost for so long, except for anyone who had been through medical school. This was actually the second such occurrence of a medical student in the last month. The other student was still missing, but no one had noticed. He was last seen in Area 51 of the basement.

"That's fantastic," Camus sarcastically retorted. "I want you to go see the three patients at the end of the hallway, and then come tell me which one has leprosy. I think you'll be pleasantly surprised."

Camus shared a gleeful and sincere grin as he said that last line.

Chapter Nine
How Long Can
Dr. Camus Hold Out?

Later that day, around three pm, Camus had a serious and sudden existential crisis (or, as he would likely have erroneously called it, an 'experimental' crisis). He was only in his mid-thirties and had completely changed who he was just two weeks before, but it didn't matter. He was pensive about what his future would be.

"I used to be happy, didn't I? Even when I was miserable, I was still happy...I think," he ruminated to himself.

A few people looked at him funny in the cafeteria as he had this full, audible conversation with himself, but at least he didn't switch sides of the table each time he responded to himself.

"How is it that two weeks ago I was excited and ready to return to medicine, but now I'm already burned out again? What's wrong with me? I almost feel like cursing somebody out, but I don't dare without the Censor here.

"I can't leave medicine because I've still got student loans to pay. No one else would hire me for anything, anyway. I had to trick my way into *this* job. So what's next? Do I just keep going and hope that I won't be too miserable? I thought being a doctor would be more exciting, like on television where I'm a hero and get my pick of the women who work at the hospital, but I'm neither good at what I do nor liked by...anybody. I hear there are lots of opportunities in places like Arizona; at least it's a dry heat.

"Maybe I *am* just a cliché? At least I didn't get this way by hitting my head, then I'd be a trope as well.

"What will my epitaph say? 'Here lies a man who couldn't go anywhere without being censored'? How absurd am I?!

"I guess I can always go back to the family business of making those stick-figure-family window decals. Or I could finally create that rock concept album I've always wanted to, about an unemployed man who writes the next great American novel. Or fake my death and ride a motorcycle around the country. That's not a bad idea.

"Perhaps I'm overthinking it. I never used to overthink anything, I mainly *under-thunk* things. I might be less troubled if I just went back to being a terrible person, 'cause trying to be good to people is killing me."

Camus sat with his head in his hands for a while. He felt like crying, but held back when he realized it might make his character too sympathetic to you, dear reader. Instead, he sat watching a guy at the next table trying to make balloon animals with his bubble gum. The Bubble Gummer looked back at Camus.

"You look familiar to me. Do I know you?"

"No," answered Camus flatly.

"You must just have one of those faces, I guess."

"No, I don't. You wanna know why? Because those faces don't exist. That's just something that stupid people say to avoid looking even dumber."

Camus couldn't believe these words came out of his mouth. He hadn't said anything so mean or crass since the hypnotism. Camus had to leave. He remembered that he left the student upstairs on his own, and needed to teach him something about leprosy. And then send him to the ED to admit all the patients piling up. And then write all of his patient notes so that the hospital could get paid. If nothing else, Camus was firmly dedicated to education.

• • •

"Well, what do you think of our patients, Future Doctor Whatever Your Name Is? Which one has leprosy?"

Camus was really trying to pull himself together for just a little longer, though the med student was still completely disheveled both inside and out; Camus hadn't even thought to let him go home and rest. He was a student. He wanted more than anything to be here and learn, right? Right?! (The answer is no.)

His eyes still wide and staring at a single spot over Camus's shoulder, as though looking at the entire absurd void of existence, the student answered with a single word: "Doonboggle!"

"What?" asked a befuddled Camus.

"Oh wait, sorry. BOONDOGGLE!"

Camus immediately felt as though a train had hit him, though it was actually just the electric floor mopper the janitor was using. All thoughts and memories and incantations of the fateful night the Amazing Ralph hypnotized him mere weeks before danced before his eyes like a million flashes of broken light. He thought for a moment that he was having a flashback from a bad acid trip. (Please note that he is contractually obligated by the author of this story not to engage in any drug use during the writing of this ditty.) The same abyss that the student saw opened before him, one that carried across the entire universe and back again, until it punched him in the face. Actually, it was Nurse Man Dennis who hit him, only because he saw the opportunity finally to do so. In that split second, when Camus's life in medicine flashed all at once, he began to live his conscious life again.

What happened next has been described in a thousand different ways, by a thousand different people, most of whom were not even present. The curses emitted from Dr. Camus rang through the entire city, slapping the face of everyone who heard them. Some were in awe of the unique verbal configurations, while others were instantly offended by the sheer quantity of words used. Some patients had heart attacks from the force of his built up ire. An orthopedic patient of Dr. Sapient pulled a muscle when hearing the racket. Ms. Smith fell out of her wheelchair, and a visiting family member slipped on a banana peel in the cafeteria. And a very distinct and loud Wilhelm Scream vanished quickly in the near foreground.

Camus was making up for lost time—all of those precious minutes over the last couple of weeks lost!—and many feel that he more than made up for it all in that single tirade. Across the whole town, dogs howled, cats meowed ferociously as though they were lions, sheep bleated mightily (Do sheep "bleat"? I don't know what else they would do. I'm pretty sure they bleat. That's what I would do if I were a sheep.), and stars began falling from the heavens, dripping down like a person fresh from showering going around the house for a towel. And the Censor was nowhere to be found to clean up the mess.

Chapter Ten
Nope, Dr. Camus
is Definitely a Jerk

Rosencrantz the CEO was enjoying a nice afternoon massage in his office when Camus's outburst echoed throughout the C-suite. He fell off of the table, assuming it was an earthquake, or possibly a meteor, or maybe even Dennis gargling again, spelling the end of his days. Not one moment beyond his realization that it was Camus making such a ruckus, he knew what needed to be done, in fact what all good, powerful leaders would do in such a situation: tell The Don to take care of it.

. . .

Dr. Don Doff took nearly two minutes to arrive—almost an eternity when having to hear such atrocious lashings—as he was enjoying an afternoon brandy in his office. At first the aria playing on his stereo drowned out Camus's emanations, but it didn't take long for the ear-splitting sound to overtake Pavarotti.

"Jacksonian Democracy Camus, what is the meaning of this?" Doff shouted in his best paternalistic tone upon arriving at the scene.

But Camus couldn't even hear him.

"Why do you bray with such fervor, you deplorable beast? Are you not aware of how such repulsive prattling damages the puissance of our customers... er... patients?! This is surely not becoming of such an arresting community fixture, *especially* in Anytown, USA, which we all know is the locus of this hospital!" Doff bellowed, his jowls shaking humorously.

Camus became silent for a moment, tilted his head, and with furrowed brow, looked at Doff askance, as if processing what Doff was saying. But the silence lasted only a few seconds before Camus decided he didn't care about his confusion over Doff's language and picked up right where he left off.

• • •

Blaine had been at home for the last week trying to save his livelihood. He was searching for any job opportunities he could find, but no other hospital was stupid enough to have a censor for troubled doctors. The stress of a looming personal financial crisis put an extra strain on his marriage, so he made his wife Mitsi sleep on the couch. (At least he let her have the highest-thread-count blanket.) The kids were on edge, sensing the dramatic shift in dad's tone and behavior. Even Birdy McBirdFace, the family parrot, stopped saying BLEEP when she realized it brought a tear of rage to Blaine's eye.

Just as Blaine was about to smash their Ming vase for comfort, the phone rang.

"Blaine! Blaine, honey! It's the hospital! They say it's urgent," Mitsi said in her high-pitched caw as she ran in a stutter-step towards him, eyebrows raised and mouth agape.

Blaine figured it was the ultimate call, the one that would finally end his career.

"What?!" he spewed into the phone in a huff.

"Blaine! Blaine! You've gotta get down here! Camus has snapped. Do you hear me? He's SNAPPED! He all of a sudden started cursing and yelling and carrying on like the old days! I can't calm him, I...I...I don't know what to do! We need you to come down and fix this!"

"Who is this?" Blaine asked half innocently and half teasingly.

"Oh, sorry, I guess I didn't say. It's Rosencrantz the CEO. You know, from The NordicTrack Forward Crescendo Care Code Red Amicus Health Priority Catalyst Wellness Memorial Hospital of His Fatherly Mediocrity? Apologies for the confusion. I figured you'd just know it was me."

"Oh, no problem. But tell me again what's going on? There's a lot of yelling in the background and I can't make out what you're saying."

"JUST GET OVER HERE NOW! I NEED YOUR HELP!"

The Censor hung up with a huge smile and a sense of relief as deep as the Marianas Trench. (I guess we can say that...can't we? Does relief go deep or wide or...or something else? Well, if you don't get the idea, then we don't want you as a reader of our fair story, anyway. I should have made that clear from the beginning.)

"Mitsi, I'm baaaaack!" he said in a very *Poltergeist* way as his face contorted into a diabolical grin.

Chapter Eleven
The End(s)

"Hey, you know how the movie *The Return of the King* had, like, a dozen endings? That would be cool to do that with this story," thought the Censor out loud.

"No, it [BLEEP] wouldn't."

. . .

"I don't get it, why did that [BLEEP] student say 'boondoggle'? It was a complete [BLEEP] non sequitur."

Camus was fairly sad that he did not remain in the life driven by his subconscious, but deep down, you might even say subconsciously, he was glad to be back to his previous self, which was quite confusing to both his conscious AND subconscious selves. Neither now knew what they truly wanted. The Censor calmed him in mere minutes, but Camus's head was still spinning from the abrupt change to his psyche.

"Don't you get it? How dense are you? I obviously put him up to it. I'm the only one around who knew that the secret word was 'boondoggle', and I was about to lose my job. When *you're* a decent human being, then *my* life falls apart. I had to get you back to the jerk you really are!"

The Censor really couldn't believe that Camus didn't figure this out on his own. But really, Camus was distracted by the thought of "Non sequitur" as a great album name by the (as yet) imaginary band Subhuman Sausage.

"I need this job. Do you think my skills translate into *any* other field? The Censor Guild is reporting that jobs in our field are dropping like flies since society learned to say whatever they want with that 'covfefe' crap."

The Censor had a look of fire and pleading in his eyes when he spoke to Camus.

"You!...you...[BLEEP BLEEP] sabotaged me! You little [BLEEP]!" But Camus immediately changed his mind. "Oh, wait, I think I actually prefer being a jerk again. Never mind. Thanks for watching out for me, buddy."

"Don't mention it. Now let's go terrorize some people."

. . .

"So how was your [BLEEP] massage?" Camus said with a wry grin.

"Oh, Camus. What would my life be like without you?" pondered Rosencrantz the CEO. "Things would be so much easier! I would've already been promoted beyond this stupid Peloton Crescendo whatever hospital! I wouldn't have to have headaches all the time. That's why I get the massages, because of the tightness I get from your absurd antics. I thought we had figured some things out. You were a changed man, penitent, actually helping people." Rosencrantz the CEO meant Camus was helping *him* by working without pay since he came back.

"You were acting more like the Chosen One, which, as we've established, is what you are."

"Again, I'm not Phil. *He's* the [BLEEP] Chosen One, not me. I can't compete with him. Or his wife, evidently," Camus disputed. But Rosencrantz the CEO wasn't listening as he didn't want to be interrupted in his rant.

"But you're just so annoying, Camus! You're not even a little gnat that won't leave. You're a BIG gnat that won't leave! Like a...a...horsefly that's stuck in my office, bumping against the window, then biting me!"

"You sound like you're speaking from a specific experience with a [BLEEP] horsefly," jabbed Camus.

"Yes! I am! You know why? Because you *are* a horsefly! You're big, and you make buzzing noises, and you keep bumping into the window!"

Rosencrantz the CEO still didn't understand irony, or how analogies worked. Or health care.

"I can't kill you with a fly swatter because you're too big. If I spray you with poison, it will stink up my office. All I can do is open the door and window and hope that you fly out. But you never do! You stay forever! Not only that, but you *enjoy* making my life miserable! I now have to spend a bunch of time convincing the board to fire you, and then all the headache *that* leaves in finding a replacement. You know how hard and expensive that is? We save money by continuing to employ you here, where you do a terrible job, and by employing this buffoon of a man to censor you in hopes of decreasing malpractice suits!"

"Didn't we already go through this [BLEEP] expedition in the first act?"

A quick elbow forcefully nudged him in the ribs.

"'Exposition' you idiot, not 'expedition'," offered the Censor, still trying to cover up for all of Camus's mistakes.

Camus just elbowed him back, but much harder.

"Did you know the board has already suggested holding a funeral for the 'new' you? They thought people would be so sad to see your old self return that we could have a service. People would say nice things;

they could mourn the return of the jerk. It might be good for morale, you know? But no one had anything to say! Even when you were *nice,* they still despised you. Dr. Sapient, who has been asking for you to be fired for at least a year, by the way, was *still* requesting it even when you were a decent human."

"So what are you [BLEEP] saying? Am I fired? Or what?"

"Not yet," stammered Rosencrantz the CEO forlornly. "But you know those pictures of people hanging out on cranes hundreds of feet in the air without a harness from the 1920s? That's what I'm going to do to you if you don't make some serious changes!"

"Okay, whatever. You [BLEEP] know that you can never get rid of me! I'll take my case right to the [BLEEP BLEEP] medical board! I'm stuck here working with [BLEEP] suckers like you, and isn't that the real crime?"

As Camus and the Censor began to leave Rosencrantz the CEO's office, Camus remembered he had one more item to get the CEO's goat. (What kind of saying is that? It's so stupid. Rosencrantz the CEO didn't even have a goat anymore! And why would getting it be such a big deal? You Americans are so outlandish.)

"Oh, and by the way, [BLEEP] Ms. Smith said she's going to sue for damages when she fell out of her

[BLEEP] wheelchair during my screaming," said Camus with no hint of remorse.

And with that, Rosencrantz the CEO morosely walked to a sign on the wall of his office, erased the number "23", and replaced it with a "0" in front of the words "Days Since Last Malpractice Suit." The longest streak of his career had now ended.

. . .

"Say it ain't so, Camus," whined an unknown little boy in the hallway outside of Rosencrantz the CEO's office.

"Sorry Jimmy. You need to learn that the world is full of two types of folks—[BLEEP] jerks, and nice people. If you stick around long enough, you'll find that those are often the [BLEEP BLEEP] same people."

"Why do you swear so much? And my name's not Jimmy."

"Shut up and go home, kid."

. . .

"So what is this, Camus? A satire? A farce? A spoof? I mean, what have we been doing here for the last however many pages?"

"I don't [BLEEP] know, Blaine. I don't [BLEEP] know. But at least it didn't have a dozen endings."

About The Author

Kyle Bradford Jones, MD is a very handsome man who practices family medicine in Salt Lake City, Utah. He is the author of *Fallible: A Memoir of a Young Physician's Struggle with Mental Illness*, winner of the 2020 Pencraft Award for Autobiography. He is enchanted by moonlit walks on the beach, decorative spoons, and Koosh balls. He is tolerated by his wonderful wife and four kids.

Note From the Author

Word-of-mouth is crucial for any author to succeed. If you enjoyed *HOSPITAL!*, please leave a review online—anywhere you are able. Even if it's just a sentence or two. It would make all the difference and would be very much appreciated.

Thanks!
Kyle Bradford Jones

We hope you enjoyed reading this title from:

BLACK ✿ ROSE
writing™

Subscribe to our mailing list—*The Rosevine*—and receive **FREE** books, daily deals, and stay current with news about upcoming releases and our hottest authors.

Scan the QR code below to sign up.

Already a subscriber? Please accept a sincere thank you for being a fan of Black Rose Writing authors.